FORE PLAY

Acclaim for Julie Cannon's Fiction

In *Smoke and Fire…*"Cannon skillfully draws out the honest emotion and growing chemistry between her heroines, a slow burn that feels like constant foreplay leading to a spectacular climax. Though Brady is almost too good to be true, she's the perfect match for Nicole. Every scene they share leaps off the page, making this a sweet, hot, memorable read."—*Publishers Weekly*

Breaker's Passion is…"an exceptionally hot romance in an exceptionally romantic setting. …Cannon has become known for her well-drawn characters and well-written love scenes."—*Just About Write*

In *Power Play…*"Cannon gives her readers a high stakes game full of passion, humor, and incredible sex."—*Just About Write*

About *Heartland…*"There's nothing coy about the passion of these unalike dykes—it ignites at first encounter and never abates. …Cannon's well-constructed novel conveys more complexity of character and less overwrought melodrama than most stories in the crowded genre of lesbian-love-against-all-odds—a definite plus."
—Richard Labonte, *Book Marks*

"Cannon has given her readers a novel rich in plot and rich in character development. Her vivid scenes touch our imaginations as her hot sex scenes touch us in many other areas. *Uncharted Passage* is a great read."—*Just About Write*

By the Author

Come and Get Me

Heart 2 Heart

Heartland

Uncharted Passage

Just Business

Power Play

Descent

Breakers Passion

Rescue Me

I Remember

Smoke and Fire

Because of You

Countdown

Capsized

Wishing on a Dream

Take Me There

The Boss of Her (Novella)

Fore Play

FORE PLAY

by
Julie Cannon

2018

FORE PLAY

ISBN 13: 978-1-63555-102-0

This Trade Paperback Original Is Published By
Bold Strokes Books, Inc.
P.O. Box 249
Valley Falls, NY 12185

First Edition: May 2018

Credits
Editor: Shelley Thrasher
Production Design: Susan Ramundo
Cover Design By Sheri (graphicartist2020@hotmail.com)

Acknowledgments

Again, it takes a village to create the end product you're reading, and there are too many people to mention. However, a special shout out to Erin for her eagle eye.

Dedication

For my family

CHAPTER ONE

"S ee ya soon, baby."
    Peyton didn't turn around or even acknowledge the voice as she walked down the wide corridor.

"You'll be back," the voice said confidently, then ended the statement with a familiar, spine-tingling cackle.

Step after step took her farther away from this place, this hellhole, her home for the past nine years, two months, and eight days. She wasn't looking back because she didn't need reminders. She would never forget the chipped cement floors, block walls with peeling paint, the three-inch-thick reinforced windows, the hard, metal beds bolted to the floor with a thin mattress, scratchy blankets, and wafer-thin pillows. Almost every metal sink faucet in the place dripped, and the steel toilets were missing their lids. She never needed to worry about putting the seat down—there was none. Small tables were bolted to the floor below a four-foot shelf hanging crooked on the wall above the desk. Redecorating was not an option.

She had nothing in her hands as she moved silently over the floor. She'd walked in with just the clothes on her back and was walking out the same way, albeit forty-two pounds lighter. Habit and discipline made her stay on the right side of the four-inch-wide black stripe that ran the length of the corridor. She was leaving catcalls, well wishes, drama, conflict, mayhem, and bullshit. No more roommates who farted, barfed, and couldn't stop talking or crying. Behind her were liars, cheaters, dopers, and those that would sell their body for a bar of soap—or to survive.

She'd had a first-row seat when pissed-off inmates threw feces at guards, spat on each other, and stuck each other with shanks made from an old toothbrush or comb. She'd witnessed beatings and heard things she'd never forget. No more strip searches, cell searches, and cavity searches. Three thousand, three hundred, fifty-four days subjected to being poked and prodded with black batons from impatient guards or those who got their power fix over those that had none. Three thousand days of nonstop noise. Even in the dark of the night when the lights were out, it was never quiet. Crying, coughing, talking, or fucking—it never stopped. Three thousand days of rising to a horn, eating, showering, and even shitting to a horn like trained animals or Pavlov's dog—basic behavioral training.

Each step took her closer to fresh air, clean clothes, and hot, delicious food. Where she could lie on a soft bed, with fluffy pillows and clean sheets. A closet full of Nike shoes, Levi's, and Ralph Lauren. Where she could have private phone conversations and hot showers any time she wanted. Every step, every foot, every yard brought her nearer a place where she could see warm smiles, hear genuine laughter, and enjoy loving faces around the table.

She stopped in front of a battered gray door, the lock as large as her fist. The man beside her sadistically took his time selecting the right key to slide noisily into the keyhole. The click of the bolt retracting was quieter than when it had slammed home behind her nine years ago. At that time, the sound had echoed off the walls, settled deep in her gut, had never left, a constant reminder of where she was—the Nelson Correctional Institute for Women.

The thick metal door creaked loudly, like a shrill train whistle, as it swung open. She waited patiently, focusing on keeping her face expressionless and her breathing steady. She fought the urge to bolt across the threshold and out the front door. She prayed this wasn't a dream. It was the same fantasy she'd had for months after coming here. The ones she'd had in the last few months were similar but ended with the door slammed in her face—cruel, vicious laughter coming from every direction.

Peyton was poked one more time on her back, just above her kidney, this time much harder than necessary. Were they ever necessary?

"You'll be back," a harsh voice said, his tobacco breath suffocating her. "You all do." He ran his stick suggestively down the crack of her ass. "And I can hardly wait."

Chapter Two

"Fore! Shit! Goddamn it! Son of a bitch!"

"Jill, relax. It's just a game."

"You think it's a game, because you're good at it."

Leigh couldn't help but laugh at her best friend of more than twenty years. They'd met in high school at volleyball tryouts and were complete opposites. Leigh was barely five-and-a-half feet tall, Jill almost six feet, with more than a few extra pounds. Leigh was a jock, and all Jill had going for her in the athleticism department was her height. Leigh's blond hair secured in a ponytail through the back of her ball cap was a sharp contrast to Jill's jet-black, so short people often mistook her for a man. Leigh excelled in just about every sport. Jill, not so much. She had heart and she tried, but without a certain amount of skill she was just a recreational athlete.

"If you keep having that kind of reaction when you hit the ball, you'll never have fun."

"So, this is supposed to be fun? How is this fun? You hit the ball, go after it, hit it again, go after it again, hit it again. See my point?" They shouldered their bags and started walking down the fairway. Jill brushed aside her observations of the game of golf, asking, "How's the new job?"

Leigh didn't like talking about it, afraid to jinx it. She had just been promoted to chief information officer for Cementic, a company that after years of success had finally cracked the Fortune 500 list. She'd worked at Cementic for twelve years, starting fresh out of MIT with her master's degree in electrical engineering and information technology, as a senior programmer, working her way up the ranks to her current position. She was one of a handful of women in a senior leadership position at Cementic and, as much as she wouldn't admit it to anyone other than Jill, had been determined to crack the final glass ceiling.

"It's going okay." Five months ago, Steve, her boss at the time, had notified the board that he was retiring. To anyone who didn't understand the intricacies of successful executive transition, it typically took months to find a successor, and in the constantly changing world of information technology, profits and a high-visibility company made it that much more difficult. Finding the individual with the right skills, temperament, and personality to work in conjunction with the other leaders of the company was never easy. Leigh, along with, courtesy of the grapevine, three external candidates, had interviewed with at least seven people for the position. She was offered the job the day after her final interview.

For the past few years, Cementic had been undergoing a transformation, and they brought in several new hires to run senior leadership positions, people with levels of expertise that those who had grown up in the company did not possess. Other than one colossal failure, their strategy had been extremely successful, and Cementic profits and market share had soared. Shareholders were happy, the board was happy, the CEO was happy, and everyone wanted to stay that way.

"So, you actually play golf with those guys?"

Leigh had told Jill that all the senior staff golfed together at least twice a month. "It's not just men. Caroline is the head of HR, and I've played a few rounds with her. I play with my boss in a few weeks."

Jill punched Leigh's arm good-naturedly. "It's true. Deals really do happen on the golf course." Jill was an attorney and had always been in private practice. Her area of expertise was environmental law and not office politics.

"As much as I'd love to think that the business world has evolved beyond that in the past twenty years, you're probably right."

"Especially in the male-dominated field you're in," Jill added, like Leigh needed reminding. "So that's why you drag me out here week after week."

"Yep. If I can't use your body for money or sex, I'll use it to help me fit in with my new peers."

"You know, Leigh, you can use my body for sex any time."

"In your dreams," Leigh replied, giving Jill her own teasing punch on the shoulder. It was an ongoing joke between them. They'd started out as friends and would never be anything other than just that. They had no sexual attraction and certainly no sexual chemistry between them. They'd seen each other through more girlfriends than they cared to count, been with each other reveling in the excitement and happiness of new love, cried on each other's shoulder in heartbreak, and shared a gallon of Rocky Road ice cream as they bashed the girl who had just broken their heart. Leigh had been Jill's maid of honor in her wedding several years ago.

"Are you still seeing Tiffany?" Jill asked, lining up her next shot.

"Pay attention to what you're doing," Leigh said, not wanting to talk about her last girlfriend.

Jill settled her feet the appropriate shoulder-length apart and adjusted her hands on the grip of her club, looking from the ball to the pin one hundred and twenty yards in front of her. Jill's first shot had gone wide of the fairway, and she'd be lucky to get her second anywhere near the green. Looking back at the ball she said, "Way to change the subject, Leigh," just before her 5 iron connected with the ball.

"Yeah, baby," Jill exclaimed, raising both arms, her club flailing over her head. "That's what I'm talking about."

Leigh shook her head. "See. What did I tell you? Don't take it so seriously, and look how well you do."

They walked another fifty yards, and Leigh pulled her 8 iron from her bag, settled in front of the ball, swung, and connected solidly with her ball. She watched it sail to the green in a perfect approach shot, landing approximately ten feet from the cup.

"So, are you going to answer my question or not?" Jill asked, knowing enough golf etiquette to not ask while she was taking her shot.

"Not."

"Why not? I thought you said she was hot and a rocket in bed?"

"I said she was very pretty and very attentive."

"Pretty, hot, attentive, rocket, same difference."

Leigh rolled her eyes at the euphemisms Jill had chosen. "Because there is more to dating someone than a pretty face and skilled hands."

"There is?" Jill asked. "I never had a problem with it."

"Because that's all you were looking for. At least until you met Joyce," Leigh said, referring to her best friend's wife.

Jill stopped and looked at her, surprise on her face. "And you're looking for something else? When did this happen?"

"I'm not," Leigh said, maybe a little too defensively.

"You need a wife, you know."

Leigh glared at her. "I don't need a wife."

"See, that's the problem, Leigh. You need one. You just don't want to admit it to yourself."

"No," Leigh said carefully. "What I need—"

"What you need until then is some wild, raunchy, uninhibited, no-attachment sex. Hey," Jill said, like she'd just thought of something earth-shattering. "How about the woman we saw filling the drink coolers when we got here? She was hot."

Leigh started walking again, pulling her putter out of her bag as Jill shot a decent approach on the green, her ball, however, landing forty feet from the cup.

Leigh had to admit it had been a while since someone made her toes curl, and Jill's idea was appealing, as was the woman she described. However, hooking up with the wrong woman could jeopardize everything she'd worked for. You never knew who worked for whom, who had the ear of someone who was important in your next career step. Leigh was planning to hold her boss's job for seven or eight years before she moved on to a larger company. Maybe something in the Fortune 200.

"Am I right or what?" Jill asked as they stepped onto the sixth green.

"I don't kiss and tell."

"Bullshit, Leigh. Yes, you do. How many times have you woken me up at zero-dark-thirty telling me all about her?"

"Jesus, Jill. You make me sound like a frat boy bragging about his latest conquest."

"No. We were sorority, and you're simply sharing things with your BFF."

"Shut up and putt. You're away," Leigh said, using the term that signified Jill's ball was the farthest from the hole.

It took Jill five strokes to get her ball into the hole, whereas Leigh needed only three.

"So, what happened with Tiffany?"

"Nothing earth-shattering," Leigh finally said, knowing Jill wouldn't let up until she knew all the details. "She was a very nice woman but a bit dull. I was bored after a few weeks. She didn't have anything original to say, and the only thing we had going for us was sex, so I ended it."

Four men had just finished teeing off on the next hole as Leigh and Jill approached, so Leigh didn't say any more. When the foursome started walking toward where their balls lay, she pulled her 3 wood from the bag and removed the Mickey Mouse head cover—a gift from Jill on her thirty-seventh birthday three months ago. "Now shut up and get ready to hit the ball. And relax."

Chapter Three

Peyton pushed the accelerator pedal on her cart as the two women approached the seventh tee box.

"Beverage, ladies?"

She'd been watching the two for the last several holes, her eyes immediately drawn to the shorter of the two. She was dressed in fashionable golf attire—dark shorts and a sleeveless white top. She was much shorter than her own five feet eleven inches and had blond hair. Light freckles sprinkled across her nose, and dark Oakley sunglasses hid her eyes. Her legs were tan and muscular, and her arms showed enough definition to indicate that she spent some time in the gym. She was wearing a white ball cap to keep the sun off her face, and her ponytail was pulled through the hole in the back. There was just something sexy about a girl in a cap.

The woman was more than a weekend hacker, the term used to describe someone who played golf only on the weekend, and poorly at that. But she did have good form and, with a few tweaks, could be an excellent golfer. The other woman was taller, her Capris were green, and her T-shirt had a large Nike swoosh across the front. Her swing was awful, which had resulted in her ball going every place except in the middle of fairway or close to the cup. However, from what Peyton had seen, they were having a good time. Having fun was just as important as the final score.

Peyton had watched them tee off on the first hole earlier this morning, noting a few subtleties the blonde needed to change to make her shots more effective. She let her shoulder drop, twisted her hips too much, and needed to extend her follow-through a little more. When she pulled up beside them, and the woman turned to acknowledge her question, her heartbeat sped up.

In her position as part-time golf instructor, part-time beverage server, and general helper at the Copperwind Golf Resort, Peyton came in contact with women every day. Most were straight and some were lesbians, but she never took advantage of the opportunity in front of her. Not at work. Never at work. She needed this job too bad to screw up for, no pun intended, a simple screw.

The dark-haired woman gave the blonde a conspiratorial wink and stepped in front of her, blocking Peyton's view. "You are my savior. What do you have in terms of an alcoholic beverage?"

"I'm sorry, but we don't serve alcohol until eleven." Peyton rattled off the selections from the dozens, if not hundreds of times she'd heard the same question. Little did they know that the resort kept meticulous records of the drinks their guests ordered, cross-referencing them to the names on dinner or golf reservations. Peyton reviewed the pairings for the day and always stocked their favorite beverage on her cart. These women were Leigh Marshall and Jill Bailey, and they both drank Diet Coke. However, she didn't know which woman was which.

"I'll have a Diet Coke," the woman said, confirming Peyton's research on their preferences. She turned to the blonde. "Since you're winning, Leigh, you're buying. And you make a lot more money than I do," she added.

The blonde, now identified by process of elimination, was Leigh Marshall. She shook her head at her friend, and her genuine smile lit up her face.

Peyton choked on her breath and immediately felt the heat of embarrassment creep up her neck as she struggled to breathe.

"Are you okay?" Leigh asked.

"Yes, fine," Peyton was able to croak out, the heat on her face increasing. Regaining her composure, she stepped out of the cart and walked to the back of the cart, where four Igloo coolers contained the drinks.

"She'll have the same." Jill used her thumb like a hitchhiker and motioned to Leigh.

Peyton reached over the cooler directly in front of her, lifted the lid, and reached inside. The action was habitual, but she knew it drew attention to the curve of her ass and her thirty-eight-inch-inseam legs. It generated large tips from the lesbians, equally generous ones from the men, and more than a few dirty looks from their wives. Peyton didn't care. The last ten years she'd learned a lot of very, very useful things, one of which she used several times a day in her role, affectionately known on golf courses around the country, as the beer babe. Since the terms of her parole prohibited her from selling alcohol, she was the beverage babe. The tips were cash, unaccounted to the IRS, and went directly into her safe for just that—safekeeping.

"Thanks," Leigh replied, exchanging a twenty-dollar bill for the cold cans. Ice slid down the side of one of the cans. Peyton reached into her pocket to make change.

"Keep it." Jill waved off Peyton's actions. Leigh's head snapped toward her friend, and Peyton saw the look that she was too polite to voice. Even she had to admit a fourteen-dollar tip for two sodas was a bit excessive. Peyton was about to say as much, when a whistle and a wave from the men on the green to her left caught her attention.

"It's fine. Thank you," Leigh said. "Catch up with us later?"

"Certainly. Thanks again. Enjoy your game," Peyton replied, not wanting to leave. But it wasn't like they all planned to chat for the rest of the afternoon. Her job was done, and she needed to move on.

"She's cute," Jill commented, tipping her head in the direction of the cart driving away. "Speaking of wild, raunchy sex—"

"Yes, she is," Leigh said. A word other than cute came to mind to describe the woman, but she refused to say that to Jill. If she did, she'd be deflecting Jill's dare for her to ask the woman out. She wasn't in the market for a girlfriend, but then Leigh realized that was a huge leap from having a quickie with the beverage babe, however drop-dead gorgeous she was. "But no."

Peyton was much taller than her, close to six feet, and she obviously spent a lot of time in the sun. Her legs were long and tan, her clothes perfectly pressed and neat. She couldn't see her eyes behind her Ray Ban sunglasses, but Leigh felt her piercing gaze. Her hair was very short, but she didn't look overly butch.

"Her name tag said Peyton. Did you see the scar on her face?" Jill asked, her voice unnecessarily quiet. Peyton was at least fifty yards away now.

Leigh had noticed and had tried not to stare at the jagged line that ran from just beside Peyton's left eye, down her cheek, and ended at her jawline. "Yes, I did. It's hard to imagine that a plastic surgeon wouldn't have sewn up a cut like that." The scar wasn't ugly, but it was noticeable.

"I suppose." Jill shook her head in agreement. "It makes her look dangerous, in a sexy kind of way." Jill raised and lowered her eyebrows to emphasize her point. "Wild, crazy sex," Jill muttered under her breath loud enough for Leigh to hear.

CHAPTER FOUR

Peyton parked her cart and handed the key to her relief. She had a lesson in thirty minutes and wanted a chance to review her notes before Steve Albert arrived. Steve, a newly minted cardiologist, was still under the misguided belief that all doctors played golf on Wednesdays. Peyton's brother-in-law Phil, a neurosurgeon, had told her that with today's health-care reimbursements, most doctors couldn't afford to take Wednesdays off anymore.

"How's business?" her brother Marcus asked when she stepped into the small office in the clubhouse. Marcus was thirty-one and looked like a young John Wayne, complete with a six-foot, four-inch frame. While Peyton was in Nelson, Marcus had married Olivia, who, at no taller than four feet ten inches, was as energetic and exuberant as the Energizer Bunny. After meeting Olivia, Peyton had wondered how in the hell they had sex, then quickly shut that thought down. She didn't need that image in her head.

Marcus had met Olivia soon after Peyton went to Nelson. They'd been dating for a few years before he brought Olivia along on one of his visits. Olivia was warm and chatted constantly and obviously loved her brother. Marcus came alone for one visit and told Peyton he wanted to propose.

"I want to spend the rest of my life with Olivia," he said nervously. "I love her."

"Marcus, that's awesome." When he didn't reply or even answer, she said, "So, what's the problem?" Peyton knew there was more to the visit than he'd let on so far.

Marcus squirmed in his hard, plastic seat, and Peyton figured it out. She touched the thick glass separating them.

As a maximum-security prisoner, visiting day consisted of both parties sitting on hard round stools separated by bullet-resistant glass. The only way they could communicate, other than by using sign language, was through a telephone handset mounted on the wall beside them. Peyton knew all conversations were monitored when, during one of her parents' early visits, an inmate slammed the phone back in its cradle and started shouting obscenities to the guards. She was taken away in handcuffs, still screaming about her rights to talk to whoever she wanted about whatever she wanted. Peyton, at first shaken by the ugly scene, quickly put it out of her mind. She had only fifteen minutes before the next inmate would occupy her seat.

"Marcus, I don't expect, nor do I want, anyone to stop living their lives just because I'm in here. Your life needs to go on, and that includes being happy. If Olivia makes you happy, then you better marry her as soon as you can." Peyton's voice was firm. "Life is too short."

Marcus's marriage to Olivia had created a partnership with his new father-in-law as part owner of the exclusive club. When Marcus wanted to give Peyton a job after she was released, his father-in-law had adamantly refused. Olivia, Marcus had told her one afternoon as they were drinking iced tea on the patio, had stood up to her father and told him that Marcus would be hiring her, and that was the end of that discussion.

Peyton owed everything to Marcus and Olivia and would never do anything to make them regret their support when no one wanted to hire an ex-convict, especially a murderer. With her background as a collegiate golfer, she knew more than enough to be a competent resident pro. Copperwind charged one hundred and ten dollars an hour for a private lesson, and Peyton took home sixty of it. She currently had twelve regular clients and at least four or five others throughout the week.

"Good. Everyone's keeping up. There was a backlog on eleven, but the foursome let the group behind them play through, and that moved things along." In addition to her beverage duties, she reported back to Marcus about how the pairings were moving through the holes. Nothing killed the reputation of a course more than golfers griping about how they had to stand around on a tee waiting for the group in front of them to clear the hole.

"We have quite a few women playing today." Marcus was determined to increase the number of women in the clubhouse and had designed several specific programs especially for them to encourage membership.

"There was a pretty good pairing out there. Bailey and Marshall, I think." Peyton knew exactly the names but didn't want to give anything away to Marcus.

"They come in a few times a month. Marshall comes in during the week too and hits a couple buckets of balls," he said, referencing the practice range. "She's not too bad."

Peyton nodded, not wanting to comment too much. "She needs a little work, but she's better than most." Peyton changed the subject. "The LGBT invitational is coming up. You ready?"

Three years ago, Marcus had started a golf tournament specifically catering to the LGBT community. He'd posted fliers in the bars and community centers around town and placed ads in every newsletter or magazine he could find that catered to the community.

Peyton had volunteered to be a caddie, and Marcus would assign caddies to teams. At last count, twenty-seven teams of two or four had signed up. The entry fee of one hundred and twenty-five dollars per person provided the golfers a tournament golf shirt and cap, four drink tickets, lunch for the day, and attendance at the awards dinner Sunday evening. The winning team received a trophy and bragging rights for the year.

"I'm excited to see how it goes. It's Olivia's favorite tournament, and it's grown each year," Marcus commented.

Peyton was still getting to know her sister-in-law, but she'd liked her from their first meeting. Olivia was the perfect complement to Marcus' calm, staid personality, often finishing his sentences when she thought he took too long to finish them himself. She'd welcomed Peyton home with no hesitation and, unlike some others, never asked about her life behind bars.

"It's mine too," Marcus said. "Everybody just wants to have some fun and play golf without any hassle. Last year we had several that were transitioning from men to women, and it'll be interesting to see how they're doing this year."

Peyton looked at her brother, trying to detect if anything underlay his comment. Marcus had been twenty-one when she went away, and she was still getting reacquainted with him. She had come out to her family in her late teens, and Marcus had been her biggest supporter. He still was, and he supported the LGBT community every chance he had. But a lot had changed in the nine years she was absent from the weekly family dinner table.

Her parents, Brad, a technical writer, and Maria, the chief nurse in the busiest emergency room in the state, had aged tremendously. Worry lines were deeper, and their dark hair now more salt than pepper. They had mortgaged their house to pay for her defense. Peyton lived in an apartment above her brother's garage, and she gave her parents almost all her paycheck every week. She kept just enough for food and utilities and a few incidentals. It was the least she could do.

Her sister, Lizzy, had just turned ten when the doors of Nelson locked behind Peyton, and now that Lizzy was nineteen, Peyton hardly recognized her. In the years she was away, Lizzy had shaved her head, had six piercings in each ear, one above each eyebrow, and a bar through her nose. Tattoos started at the first knuckle on each hand and continued up her arm, shoulder, and chest as far as Peyton could see. When Peyton saw Lizzy the first time after she was released, Lizzy had told her, no, demanded, that she should address her as Elizabeth. Lizzy was a little girl's name, and she was not a little girl. Peyton and her mother often talked about the anger and guilt Elizabeth carried like one of her angry tattoos. Maria had shared with Peyton how, in one drunken episode, Elizabeth had shared that she felt overwhelming guilt for Peyton going to jail.

Her other sister, Natalie, now twenty-eight and more than a little overweight from sitting behind a desk, was just getting back into the good graces of her boss, the district attorney. She had been instrumental in petitioning for Peyton's release and had gotten her ass chewed, spit out, and handed to her because of it. Natalie's fiancé at the time of Peyton's conviction had dumped her via text the day after her sentencing. He was callous enough to ask for the ring back, and Natalie had gladly returned it somewhere inside a baggie full of dog shit from the local park. She'd since gone on to marry a neurosurgeon.

"Do you get any backlash from the other members?" Peyton asked.

"A few. Olivia told the ones who complained to get over it or go play somewhere else."

Peyton gladly added another tally mark in the "Owe" column under Olivia's name.

CHAPTER FIVE

After more than ten years, the dream was as real as it was when it happened. Every detail marched through her mind in an orderly procession.

The police came the day after the shooting and took Peyton into custody. They searched her, gave her the legally required Miranda Warning, and informed her that she had the right to remain silent and to have an attorney, and that anything she said could and would be used against her. She immediately requested a lawyer.

Peyton had taken the law into her own hands and was judge, jury, and executioner. And she was okay with that. If it brought peace of mind to her little sister, she had no conscience. She knew she'd be questioned about the killing, and she had a lawyer's phone number memorized.

She was officially booked and asked questions that she answered without her lawyer present, including her name and address, emergency contact information, and treatment for any medical condition. She was moved to another room, where her fingerprints were taken using a machine that looked like a standard copy machine. There was no ink or mess, and each of her ten fingers—her right and left four fingers and her thumbs—was digitally scanned into a database. She was handed a blackboard with white block letters spelling out her name, the date, and an identifying number and told to stand against a wall containing a measuring chart and look directly into the camera. The light was harsh, and the flash blinded her for a few seconds.

She was taken to a small, empty room and told to remove all her clothes. One of the two female guards in the room watched Peyton as she stripped, the other taking her clothes and thoroughly inspecting each item. Peyton knew what search was next and complied with their instructions, knowing the sooner this was over, the sooner she could get out of there.

She was taken to a holding cell and told she'd remain there until her lawyer arrived. Four other women were in the cell, each of whom looked like this wasn't their first visit. Woman #1 had dirty blond hair that looked like it hadn't seen shampoo in weeks. She sat on the corner of the bench, her knees drawn up, a blank look on her face. Woman #2 was as tall as #1 and pencil-thin, her dress tight against her breasts and stomach. Her legs were disproportionately smaller than the rest of her, and she wore flip-flops. Number 3 had her head in the metal toilet, retching, the sound echoing off the concrete walls, the smell permeating the stale air. The last woman's shorts were too short, her top too revealing, and her heels too tall for anyone other than a hooker. She was sitting on the other end of the bench from #1, examining her nails like she was just biding her time until she was bailed out.

The women looked at her when she entered, and Peyton made eye contact with each of them. It was her way of saying don't fuck with me. It either worked or they just didn't care and left her alone.

Her lawyer, Bernard Lerner, showed up an hour later, and she was led, in handcuffs, to an interview room. When they were left alone, as required by law, Peyton went over exactly what she'd done step by step. Lerner peppered her with questions and after two hours left her with strict instructions to not say a word to anyone about anything without him present. She returned to the holding cell, where this time, only woman #3 remained, and five new occupants were there. She received the same once-over and silent treatment as before.

Several hours later, she and the other women were taken, again in handcuffs, this time secured to a chain around their waist, to a courtroom and instructed to sit in metal folding chairs in what looked like a jury box. The proceedings began, and one by one the women, along with their attorneys, faced the judge. Each one's case number and charges were read for the record, and when asked how they pled, they all claimed their innocence. When Peyton's name was called, she calmly stood beside Lerner and, under his specific direction, repeated that she too was pleading innocent. This had been a major argument between her and Lerner. Peyton fully intended to accept whatever was the punishment for her actions. Lerner had finally convinced her to plead innocent and said that he would explain everything to her later.

Her attorney successfully argued that she was not a flight risk nor a risk to society, and her bail was set at three million dollars. It took another few days for her parents to post her bail, and it was well after noon the following day when she was released to a media frenzy.

The anticipation of a trial polarized the community, the nation, and even as far away as South Africa. There was an equal split between those who wanted to see all charges dropped and those who wanted Peyton burned at the stake. People holding signs bearing the words VIGILANTE and MURDERER in bold, block letters jockeyed for position with those that were equally supportive crowding the steps to the courthouse. Microphones were stuck in her face, and, if not for her father and her lawyer, she would not have been able to move through the throngs of people on the sidewalk.

After weeks of negotiations between the prosecutor and her attorney, Peyton pleaded guilty to voluntary manslaughter. The judge sentenced her to fifteen years in prison, and the heavy metal door, and her life, slammed behind her.

Peyton sat up in bed, her breathing ragged, sweat dripping off her forehead. It took a few moments for her to realize she was in her own bed, not a cold, hard cot in a skanky cell. She got up and turned on the lights in her apartment, quietly chanting the mantra she'd created in Nelson to calm herself. She murmured one word per step, with fifteen steps in total. Back and forth she walked across her apartment until her heart rate slowed and her breathing returned to normal. She knew she wouldn't be able to fall back asleep, so she sat down at her kitchen table and opened her well-worn deck of cards. She found it ironic that she played solitaire for hours.

CHAPTER SIX

Peyton, I need to fill in a foursome," Marcus said.

Peyton stepped away from the counter and looked at her brother.

"We've had a last-minute scratch, and the group is asking for a single. We had one, but he's already paired up."

Peyton sighed. As much as she loved playing, she'd rather get her tips from the cart. She needed the money. "Sure," she said easily. Marcus needed her, and she wasn't going to let him down. "Let me get my gear."

She hustled to her truck and pulled her golf bag and shoes from the passenger side. The clubs clanged together as she hefted the strap of the bag over her shoulder and shut the door. She hurried back to the clubhouse, mentally preparing for the round she was about to play.

A few minutes later she joined her foursome on the first tee. Their tee time was in eight minutes, but she wanted to at least introduce herself before then. As she approached the group, two of the team looked vaguely familiar.

One of the women looked her way and smiled expectantly. "Are you our fourth?"

"Yes. Peyton." She extended her hand to the woman. She was an attractive woman in her mid-forties, dressed in a royal-blue Nike golf shirt and white capris.

"Hilde Rochelle." The woman shook Peyton's hand and almost crushed it, her grip so tight. "This is Jill and Leigh." She introduced the other women, and Peyton was surprised and pleased to see Leigh Marshall was one of them.

"We've met," Leigh said, shaking her hand. "But not officially." Tingles ran up Peyton's arm, and her pulse picked up.

"You've been holding out on us, Leigh." Hilde's eyes moved up and down Peyton's body. "We'll be expecting all the details over cocktails."

Leigh had the politeness to blush at the innuendo. "It's not like that. Peyton, uhh...uhh...works here," she said finally. "Jill and I met her a couple of weeks ago."

Peyton had gotten very good at reading people and what was between the lines, and she detected more than a little unease in Leigh. Obviously, she didn't want Hilde to know she drove the beverage cart. Fine with her. She didn't need their approval. They could judge her on her game instead.

"What do you do?" Hilde asked, the look in her eye conveying her renewed interest now that it was clear it wasn't like "that" between her and Leigh.

"I'm one of the pros," Peyton answered. Out of the corner of her eye she could see Leigh's surprise.

Hilde stepped close to Peyton, running her fingernail down her arm. As she passed she said, "I'll bet you could teach me a thing or two."

Peyton looked at Leigh and was surprised to see anger flare in her eyes before disappearing as fast as it had arrived.

"Jesus, Hilde. Give it a break," Jill said, placing her neon-orange golf ball on her tee. "Let's play. Loser buys the first round."

It was clear to everyone that Hilde was not going to give it a break, and after missing her birdie putt on the fifth green, Peyton pulled her aside.

"I appreciate your interest, Hilde, but I'm not in the market for anything or anyone right now." Peyton kept her voice low and conversational. She'd mastered the art of saying something without really saying it loud enough for anyone nearby to hear.

"You're kidding, right?" Hilde replied, a look of surprise on her face.

Peyton wondered if everyone Hilde came on to fell under her spell and into the sheets with her. Since losing her freedom, Peyton preferred to be the one in control in all aspects of her life, especially her sexual partners. She was the pursuer, always went to their place, and never, ever spent the night. She had an understandable yet debilitating fear of waking up and somehow being back in prison. She felt safe in her apartment, where she could toss and turn and wake from nightmares without embarrassment—or explanation.

After almost nine months, she was still restless and slept with one eye open. At least the nightmares of her release being nothing but a dream had subsided. Now they occurred only once or twice a week instead of every night.

"If this were a different time, it might be another story, but..." She let her explanation drop, its meaning evident.

"I bet I can change your mind." Hilde's voice was husky as she stepped closer to her.

"I appreciate it, but no thanks," Peyton said strongly and hopefully clear enough.

"Hilde, for God's sake, leave her alone," Leigh said over Peyton's right shoulder.

Peyton spun around more out of defense than guilt. No one had snuck up on her in over ten years, and it shook her. How had Leigh gone from the other side of the green to right behind her without her knowing it?

"She said no, and unlike your other conquests, she probably means it."

Hilde shot daggers at Leigh before practically stomping to her ball.

"Doesn't get told no much?" Peyton asked, her nerves still on edge.

"Actually, never, at least as far as I know, or she says," Leigh added, shaking her head and watching Hilde stalk away. "Sorry about that."

Peyton waved her hand. "Don't worry about it. No big deal."

Leigh looked at her, dark eyes burning a trail up and down Peyton's body. "I'm sure you get hit on all the time. Oh, God," Leigh said, covering her face with both hands. "I didn't just *think* that, did I?"

Peyton chuckled. "Nope, and thanks."

"God, I'm so embarrassed." Leigh's hands muffled her voice.

"No need. And thank you for coming to my rescue."

"I doubt you rarely need rescuing either."

Peyton's insides warmed at the sound of Leigh's voice and the friendly, stress-free conversation. She'd had to watch what she said and to whom at Nelson, and almost as much now. No one wanted to date an ex-con, sleep with one, or even be around one. Peyton was saved from making further comment as it was Leigh's turn over the putter.

"You said you were one of the course pros. Does that mean you give lessons?" Jill asked three holes later. She squinted at Peyton through her thick-lensed prescription sunglasses as Leigh was lining up to hit her tee shot on the next hole.

"Yes, I do." Peyton had been watching Leigh swing the club for the last few holes and noted that, with some minor adjustments, she could lengthen her drive by at least twenty-five yards. With a few more changes, she could increase the loft of the ball as it traveled through the air.

"Leigh has to play a lot of golf with the people she works with, and she has a big round with the president of her company in a few weeks that she's really nervous about."

Peyton frowned, trying to see what that had to do with her previous question. "What does she do?"

"She's a big VP and does something in IT. It's too technical for me, but she's obviously really good at it."

Peyton still had no clue how this all tied together. Maybe it didn't, she thought. Maybe Jill was simply making conversation. The pace of the changes in technology since she'd been in Nelson was absolutely mind-boggling—and scary. She'd had one of the original iPhones before she went in, but Bluetooth, iCloud, and web mail were completely new to her. Her current iPhone was two models old and a hand-me-down from Olivia.

"What does she have to be nervous about? She seems rather confident and sure of herself, and she has a pretty good game." And the combination was nothing short of sexy, Peyton thought.

"They're playing here, I think. How ridiculously old-school chauvinistic is that?" Jill's question contained more than a little sarcasm. "No offense against your club."

The familiar whack of hitting the ball squarely in the center of the club was unmistakable, and Peyton watched as Leigh's ball sailed into the air. Several seconds later it landed squarely in the center of the fairway. "With a shot like that, she'll have nothing to worry about," Peyton commented.

"Maybe, but the other day she mentioned she should probably take a few lessons."

"I'm not here to solicit business, Jill," Peyton said uncomfortably. "I'm just your added fourth."

Thankfully it was her turn on the tee, effectively ending the conversation, however, not before Peyton admitted to herself she wouldn't object to spending more time with Leigh.

"You told her what?" Leigh asked, walking with Jill toward her ball. They were approaching the green on the twelfth hole.

"I was just trying to help."

"But did you have to tell her I was nervous? Why did you tell her at all?" Leigh struggled to keep her voice from carrying to Peyton, who was walking a few yards behind them.

"Because you mentioned you wanted some lessons."

"I said I was thinking I might benefit from some," Leigh said. "God. She probably thinks I'm trolling for free advice." And that possibility made her more uncomfortable than she cared to admit.

"Don't worry about it. She said she wasn't playing with us to solicit business. Chill, Leigh. She seems really cool."

Chill and cool were not the words Leigh would use to describe her body's reaction to being near Peyton. When Leigh had seen her approach them on the first tee, she knew Peyton was their fourth. She'd been more than a little surprised, having expected the beverage server to do little more than serve beverages. At least that was her experience at other courses where she'd played. Leigh had revised her narrow opinion when Peyton drove her ball farther and straighter than anyone else and had nine birdies on her scorecard. She, herself, had two bogeys, which put her two strokes behind Hilde and six ahead of Jill.

Leigh had always wondered how the scoring of golf originated. Each hole had a set number of shots that the designers believed would take the golfer to get the ball in the cup. If they made it in that number, it was called par, which made sense. Where it got squirrely was that fewer shots were called birdies and more shots were bogeys. On the previous hole, Peyton had sunk her ball in the hole in three shots instead of the set number of four, while she, Jill, and Hilde had made par.

"She must play a lot," Jill commented. "Her form is perfect. And her body isn't too bad either," she added, bumping Leigh with her hip. "I'd love to have her arms wrapped around me showing me exactly where to put my hands." Jill fanned herself with her gloved hand.

"Jesus, Jill. First Hilde, then you. It's like playing with horny teenage boys. And you're married," she added. *Like Jill needed any reminder. After two kids she was still crazy in love with her wife.*

"Just because I'm off the market, I'm not dead. Come on, Leigh. Don't tell me you haven't noticed."

Leigh had done nothing but notice, which was evidenced by her score. Peyton's swing was graceful and the intensity of her commitment to her game evident. She approached every shot the same way, looking from her ball to where the ball was going to land, then back at her ball. Leigh had the impression Peyton was visualizing exactly where she planned to place her ball. She hadn't deviated from her routine on any of her shots. Maybe that's why she was eating their lunch in this round.

"Looks like we have a crowd ahead of us."

Peyton's voice right beside her startled Leigh, and she stumbled. Thankfully Peyton caught her around the waist before she did an embarrassing face-plant.

"You okay?" Peyton asked, their bodies pressed close together. The feel of Peyton's hard body against hers sent Leigh's pulse racing and her heart running to keep up. She fit perfectly under Peyton's arm, her eyes level with Peyton's lips. Leigh watched them move as Peyton spoke. She tingled with the sensation of what they would feel like on her. She definitely needed to get laid, and soon. No, she was anything but okay, but no way in hell was she going to tell Peyton that.

Peyton released her and stepped back, but not before Leigh saw a flash of desire in her eyes.

Leigh had admittedly found Peyton extremely attractive from their very first meeting, the moment Peyton pulled up in her cart two weeks ago. Whereas most of the women that drove the cart were straight, Peyton was anything but. Judging by the confident way she carried herself and the way she made and held direct eye contact, she was obviously a lesbian. She hadn't tried to flirt to increase her tips, and her aloofness wasn't negative in a standoffish kind of way but simply showed that she was all business and didn't get too familiar with the members or their guests.

Peyton had been dressed similarly to what she was today, in knee-length golf shorts and a light-blue polo shirt with the Copperwind logo just above her left breast. She looked extremely professional and hadn't done anything to indicate otherwise in their first twelve holes. She hadn't offered any unsolicited advice to any of them about how they could improve their game, nor had she joined in the familiar camaraderie and teasing that friends do when their ball couldn't hit the cup after eight strokes. She pretty much kept to herself, and the conversation that she did join was completely appropriate.

The heat must be getting to me, Leigh thought as they dropped their bags behind a foursome that was already waiting. The players in front of that group had just teed off and were walking down the fairway. The two couples in front of them glanced over their shoulder, and Leigh detected more than a little interest as one of the women appraised their foursome, her eyes lingering a little too long on Hilde and even longer yet on Peyton. Her eyes lit up with familiarity, and Leigh felt a surge of jealousy, however unwarranted it was. There was no reason for it, it made absolutely no sense, but it was there nonetheless.

Leigh felt Peyton stiffen beside her as the woman left her group and stepped forward.

"Peyton, it's so good to see you again." Her voice had a soft, Southern drawl that reminded Leigh of Scarlett O'Hara, the heroine in the 1939 movie *Gone with the Wind.*

"Hello, Denise," Peyton replied politely. "How are you?"

"I'd be much better if you'd join our group. I'm afraid I don't play as well without you as I do with you."

The woman's meaning was more than innuendo, and for some bizarre, shocking reason, Leigh wanted to step forward and smack the smirk off the woman's face.

"I'm sure you're doing just fine."

"Oh, I am, sugar, but I'd love to be better."

Leigh couldn't believe the audacity of this woman. She was hitting all over Peyton as if they weren't even there. She had no idea if Peyton was with any of us, but then again maybe she did. Maybe she knew Peyton was single. Maybe she knew Peyton would take her up on her offer. Maybe Peyton already had, and she was looking for a repeat. But something told Leigh that wasn't the case.

"Jill, Hilde, Leigh, this is Denise Jamison, one of my clients," Peyton said, introducing them.

"Nice to meet you," Denise said, but didn't take her eyes off Peyton. Obviously, she didn't care who they were.

"Are you making notes on your game like we talked about in last week's lesson?"

"Of course, sugar. I do everything you tell me to do, and ask me to do," she added suggestively.

Her sugary drawl with emphasis on the endearment *sugar* was turning Leigh's stomach.

"Maybe we can get together at the clubhouse after we're done here, and I can divulge all my weaknesses, and you can give me some pointers."

Jill tried to stifle a laugh at the absurdity and ridiculousness of Denise's approach. Good God, Leigh thought. Why don't you just say let's meet in the clubhouse and fuck? "I'm afraid I'm not available this afternoon. We can talk about it at your lesson next week. It's Tuesday, right?"

Denise's eyes narrowed, and it appeared she was trying to decide whether to step up her verbal seduction or give up. Before Denise had a chance to make up her mind, one of the men in her group called, "Denise, you're up. Let's go."

Denise gave Peyton one more long, very obviously interested look before saying, "See you on Tuesday. I'm beside myself with anticipation."

"Wow." Jill stepped next to Peyton after Denise was out of earshot. "I don't know about you, but if she were looking at me like she was looking at you, I'd need a cold shower or a moment alone."

Peyton's head whipped around, and she glared at Jill. "I don't do that."

Jill, obviously taken aback by Peyton's sharp rebuttal, lifted her hands, palms out, in front of her. "I didn't mean anything by that, Peyton. I apologize."

Leigh watched the interchange between the two and noticed Peyton exhale and her shoulders relax. "No problem. I apologize for my overreaction. This is my job, not a place to pick up women."

"And I bet you have plenty of opportunity. I don't know if I could resist the temptation, if they look like that," Jill added.

"Then aren't you lucky you work for yourself. You should come work for me," Hilde said. "I have more women in my office than I know what to do with."

"No, thanks. Joyce would kill me," Jill said, referring to her wife and the mother of their two kids. "Peyton, how did you become a club pro?"

Peyton appeared to be relieved that the subject had changed. "I played a little golf in college. Marcus, the club manager, knew that, and here I am."

"Where did you go to school?" Jill asked.

"The tee is clear. Jill, you're up," Peyton said instead of answering the question.

"How long have you been here?" Leigh asked, wanting to know more about Peyton.

"About a year."

"Where were you before that? Were you a pro at some other club?"

"Hilde, you're up." Peyton again deftly changed the subject.

"I get the impression you don't like to talk about yourself," Leigh said, voicing her thoughts.

Peyton didn't comment on her observation. Instead, she said, "I'm here to teach golf and serve beverages."

"And occasionally make a foursome."

"And occasionally make a foursome."

"I don't even know your last name."

A wary expression crossed Peyton's face.

"I don't know yours either. Has it affected our game?"

"Marshall," she said. Peyton didn't reply. "This is where it's expected that you tell me yours."

"Well, I've never been known for doing the expected, Ms. Marshall. I believe I'm up. Excuse me." Peyton headed to the tee.

"She's a mysterious one, isn't she?" Jill commented as the waiter served their drinks. They'd finished their round, stored their clubs, changed out of their golf shoes, and were sitting at a table at the far end of the patio. A light breeze cooled the air, and the sun was far enough in its decline that they were in the shade. The putting green was to their right, the driving range to their left, and the first tee straight in front of them. Peyton had declined their invitation to join them and disappeared into a back room shortly after they came off the eighteenth green.

"That's a locked box I'd like to open," Hilde said, continuing to make known her obvious interest in Peyton.

"She's already thrown away the key, as far as you're concerned," Jill said, poking Hilde in the side playfully.

"I've picked a lock a time or two. Just makes it more of a challenge." Hilde lifted her glass of beer to her pouty lips.

"You were talking to her, Leigh. Did you find out anything?"

"No. She was pretty tight-lipped."

"Did you even get her last name?"

"No."

"Last names are rarely important," Hilde added.

"Jesus Christ, Hilde, would you give it up," Leigh snapped, judging by the reaction on her two friends' faces, completely out of character.

"What's got your panties in a wad?" Hilde asked, quickly recovering. Hilde sat back in her chair, her smile growing. "You're attracted to her."

"Hilde, I am not attracted to her." Even to Leigh's ears, her protest sounded way too strong. "Unlike you, I don't want to fuck every lesbian I see."

"That's not true," Jill said. "Hilde wants to fuck every *woman* she sees," she added, trying to inject some levity to the conversation that had suddenly become very tense. Hilde and Jill high-fived each other.

"You got that right, girl. I have only so many days until I die." She turned to Leigh. "You should try it, Leigh."

"Why is everyone so concerned about my sex life?" Leigh asked.

Hilde and Jill looked at each other. "Who else is concerned about your sex life?"

"Susan," Leigh replied, sorry she'd opened her mouth.

"What did Susan say? And don't lie. I've got your sister on speed dial, and I can call her before you even get it out of your mouth," Hilde said.

Susan, Leigh's younger sister, was a frequent guest at Leigh's house and had met most of her friends. Susan was twenty-three and thought that getting laid was the solution to just about anything. Leigh remembered those days and had to agree.

"I'll paraphrase in terms you two can understand. She said I need to get laid."

"She's right," Jill said.

"Damn right," echoed Hilde. "You're looking a little tight around the edges, and your tongue is a little sharp. In addition, you lost your patience a long time ago. I, however," Hilde spread her hands in front of her as if to say, look at me, "never display any of those unflattering characteristics. Hence, my point."

"I'm busy. I've got more important things to do than—"

"That's where you're wrong, girl. Nothing's more important than a good orgasm. Unless it's four or five." Hilde smiled smugly.

This time Hilde and Jill clinked glasses in solidarity.

"Look. I get it, and I agree with both of you. I've just got a lot on my mind, and I've been working my ass off since getting this promotion. My job is important to me. As my friends, you should understand that."

Jill laid her perfectly manicured hand on Leigh's forearm. "You know we do, Leigh. It's just that we worry about you."

"Well, don't. I'm fine. I'm happy with my life, with where I am. Once my life settles down, then I'll think about getting a girlfriend."

"Honey," Hilde said, touching Leigh's shoulder. "You need to do more than *think* about getting a girlfriend."

"I'll do more than just *think* about a girlfriend," Leigh said to end the conversation. Thankfully Jill and Hilde had turned their attention to their food that had just arrived, and they couldn't see Leigh look around for any sign of Peyton.

Chapter Seven

"Peyton, you have Marshall and Stark. John, you have..."
Peyton didn't hear the rest of the caddie assignments,
her heart skittering at the familiar name. Today was a charity golf
tournament benefitting the county's foster-care system, and Peyton
was pulling caddie duty. They had over thirty pairings today, so it
was all hands on deck for anyone requesting a caddie.

Peyton glanced down at the paper in front of her, locating the
tee time of her pair, and noticed the paper in her hands was shaking.
She set it on the table, a finger on each corner, and pushed down,
applying pressure to steady her hands. She had a little over thirty
minutes to find and meet her assignment.

Marcus finished the instructions regarding the day's events,
including the awards dinner that started at five. Peyton hustled to
the employees-only locker room and sat on one of the benches in
front of a bank of twelve floor-to-ceiling lockers. Hers was on the
far left, her name laminated in black letters four inches from the top.
Her neon-purple combination padlock hung from the handle. After
nine years of dull gray and dingy white, Peyton surrounded herself
with splashes of color wherever she could.

Too nervous to sit still, Peyton jumped back up and paced
the small room. She didn't spend a lot of time in here. It was
claustrophobically similar to the ones she'd left behind almost a
year ago. But that's where the similarities ended. That room was a
dull shade of gray, faded from years of fluorescent light and chipped

from the hundreds of women who had occupied its space. This room was a bright shade of yellow with a three-inch blue trim just below the white ceiling.

The lockers were a contrasting royal blue, the industrial-strength carpet under her feet, gray with a diamond pattern that transitioned to slip-safe tile leading into the showers, toilet, and sink area. The entire locker room was probably a thousand square feet, and nothing about it should have made Peyton feel claustrophobic other than the fact that there was one door in and out and absolutely no windows. She looked at the large clock emblazoned with the Copperwind logo high on the wall across the room. It was time to meet Marshall and Stark and determine if, in fact, Marshall was Leigh.

Peyton looked at herself in the full-length mirror and saw exactly what she'd seen when she left her apartment this morning. Her pale-blue shirt was tucked neatly into the waistband of shorts that fell just above her knees, the crease still razor sharp. She grabbed her hat, took a deep breath, and walked out.

"Where is our damned caddie?" Peter Stark asked, none too happy.

Stark was the head of the audit department for Cementic, and Leigh wasn't his original partner. Her boss, Larry Taylor, had signed up with Stark to play in the tournament, but at the last minute his grandson was hospitalized, and he and his wife had to fly to Omaha. Larry had volunteered or, more appropriately, volun-told Leigh to play in his place. Even though Leigh was happy for the opportunity to connect with a senior member of the executive team and that Larry had thought of her, Stark wouldn't have been her first, second, or even her fifth choice. He had a Napoleon complex and was at least fifty pounds overweight. He was already sweating profusely, and they hadn't even started the first hole.

Leigh looked at her watch and saw that it was twenty-five minutes past the hour, and their caddie still had a few minutes to arrive. A caddie was provided with her registration, if desired, but

Leigh preferred to carry her own bag. Stark, however, obviously did not. He was already hot under the collar.

"I'm sure he's on his way, Peter. He doesn't know us any more than we know him," Leigh said, trying to get him on a positive track.

"Well, they need to be much better organized than this."

Leigh sighed and shook her head, starting to think it was going to be a long day.

"Mr. Stark? I'm Peyton, your caddie for the day. Welcome to Copperwind. Thank you for joining us, and I hope you enjoy the event."

Leigh didn't know who was more surprised, Stark that his *he* was, in fact a *she*, or Leigh, who would be spending the next eighteen holes and several hours in the company of the woman who had provided her several very vivid and arousing dreams.

"You're a girl," Stark commented needlessly.

"Actually, Mr. Stark, I'm a woman and your caddie. Is there a problem?"

Stark frowned, his bushy gray eyebrows almost covering his eyes. He started to open his mouth, but Peyton didn't give him a chance to reply.

"Mr. Stark, Copperwind is one of the most exclusive golf clubs in the country. I can assure you I am more than qualified. We're teeing off on the first tee, which is a par five, five hundred and twenty-five yards with a dogleg to the left. I suggest, with your handicap, you should start with your driver, then your 4 iron, give or take twenty-five yards. There are bunkers in front and to the left and right of the green. The pin is in the back of the green today. A nice seventy-five-yard chip, and you can two-putt it in."

Stark's mouth dropped open as Peyton recited the statistics of the next few holes before he gathered his composure and waved her off. "Fine. Let's go. I don't want to be late."

He tossed his putter to Peyton and swiveled on his heel, digging his spikes in so much he kicked up a divot, then stomped off toward the first tee box.

Peyton lifted Stark's bag and effortlessly seated the wide strap on her shoulder. The muscles in her forearms and biceps flexed under the heavy bag.

"Good to see you again, Leigh," Peyton said after turning to her.

"He wasn't my choice to play with."

"Well, that being what it is, shall we go? We don't want to be late." She mimicked Stark's statement with a grin.

"Is there anything in this club you don't do?" Leigh asked as they walked toward the tee.

"I don't cook," Peyton replied blandly.

"I'll have to remember that." Remembering anything about Peyton had not been difficult. It had been a couple of weeks since Peyton had filled out their foursome, and on more than one occasion, Leigh had relived practically every minute like a silly schoolgirl with her first crush. She recalled the warm timbre of Peyton's voice, the way she concentrated on her game, the way she smiled, her tanned, long legs, her strong arms, and the way her shirt pulled tight across her breasts when she swung her club.

"Are any others from your company playing today?"

"No," Leigh answered, pulling her mind out of the gutter and back to the green grass in front of her. "My boss signed up and at the last minute couldn't make it."

"Well, I hope you enjoy yourself, and if there's anything I can do, don't hesitate to ask."

"I think you'll have your hands full with Stark," she said confidently, Stark had already shown he was high maintenance.

It was their turn on the tee, and Stark ignored the club Peyton offered him and pulled out an alternative one instead. *So, that's the way it's going to be. What a prick.*

He placed his ball on his tee, stepped back, looked at the fairway once, then hit the ball. His form was awful, and Leigh cringed. He didn't look to see where his ball landed. Obviously, that was Peyton's job. He stood where he was, waiting for Peyton to come to him to retrieve his club. Leigh and Stark had been paired up with two men in bright-red polo shirts with a State Farm logo, who teed off after Stark. Leigh was playing off the front tees, twenty-five yards in front of the men's. Historically, they had been referred to as the men's and women's tees, but in today's climate of political correctness and gender equality, they were simply termed the front and back. More than likely Stark didn't get that notice.

Leigh set her ball, stepped back, and took a deep breath. The first hole was always the worst, with everyone watching you before settling into their own games. She had a 1 wood, the grip comfortable in her hands. She lined up to the ball, took another deep breath, exhaled half of it, and swung.

The thwack of the club hitting the ball was indicative that she'd made good contact and hadn't embarrassed herself. Her ball sailed into the air and landed a respectable distance down the fairway. She exhaled and picked up her tee.

Echoes of "nice shot" surrounded Leigh as she replaced her club and shouldered her bag.

Leigh heard Stark's labored breathing as he walked down the fairway. If this was the way he sounded on the first hole, she was afraid he might stroke out on the back nine.

The first three holes were uneventful, and Stark continued his passive-aggressiveness by ignoring whatever club Peyton offered him. Finally, on the fourth hole, and already down by three strokes, he grudgingly accepted her recommendation and parred the hole.

There was a bottleneck on the eleventh tee, the waiting golfers exchanging money for drinks from the woman driving the beverage cart. This woman looked nothing like Peyton; however, she could have been a cocktail waitress at Hooters.

Leigh stood next to Peyton and watched six of the nine men in front of her fall all over themselves to chat her up. It was so obvious and so apparent what was going on, Leigh could only shake her head.

"Do you think it'll ever change?" she asked Peyton, who stood beside her.

"As long as there are women like that and men like that, I doubt it," Peyton replied, not even asking for clarification.

The other caddies stood huddled under a tree, each holding a can of Coke in their hand, their bags leaning against their hips. Peyton stayed beside Leigh and made no move to join them.

"You can go be with the others." Leigh waved in the direction of the other caddies.

"I'm good right here. I could say the same to you."

"I'm good right here," Leigh said and was rewarded when just the edges of Peyton's mouth turned up.

"Since this is our second date, are you going to tell me your last name now?"

Peyton's eyebrows rose, but she kept her gaze focused straight ahead. Peyton's heightened sense of her surroundings was unusual, and Leigh wanted to ask more about that, but this wasn't the time.

"Technically, this is our third, and no. Does it matter?"

Leigh's stomach tingled that Peyton remembered the first time they'd seen each other and counted that as well.

"No, but Jill and Hilde were wondering."

"Were they?"

"Yes, they were. They also wanted to know where you went to school, if you're single," and where you got that scar on your cheek, Leigh thought but didn't say.

"And if I tell you, are you going to report back to them?"

"Well, they are my friends." Leigh answered like it was a no-brainer.

Peyton smiled and nodded. "And that's what friends do."

Leigh wasn't sure if that was a question or simply a statement. "Of course," Leigh said playfully. "We tell each other everything."

Peyton slowly turned her head and looked at her. At least Leigh thought she was. The lenses of Peyton's Ray Bans were too dark to be sure exactly where she was looking.

"Everything?"

Leigh could feel the heat from Peyton's look and the innuendo in just that one word. "Well, they do...tell me everything, that is."

"And you don't?"

"No."

"And why is that?"

"Well, first of all, it's none of their business," Leigh said, then clamped her mouth shut when she realized what she was about to say.

Peyton cocked her head and lifted her eyebrows, her expression clearly saying, and…

Leigh didn't want to say anything, but her thought never made it to her mouth. "And there's nothing to talk about."

Peyton slid her sunglasses down her nose, just far enough that Leigh could see her eyes. "Nothing?"

Peyton's eyes were dark and piercing, and as much as Leigh wanted to look away, she couldn't. Their intensity hypnotized her, and she felt drawn into another place. A place she'd never been before and, for some reason, wasn't afraid to go now.

"Well, not for a while," she managed to croak out.

Peyton's eyes flashed with desire before she slid her sunglasses back up her nose, effectively creating a wall between them. She stepped away.

Leigh was shaken by her reaction to the power of Peyton's eyes and the way her inhibitions slipped away as her arousal soared. She wanted to get lost in their depth, with Peyton leading the way out, or leading her anywhere. But they held a sadness and wariness that she couldn't mask, and Leigh wanted to reach in and soothe it.

"Leigh," Stark called out from the side of the beverage cart. "If you want something to drink, you'd better get over here."

Stark's coarse voice was like fingernails on a chalkboard, and Leigh hurried over just so he wouldn't call her again. She wasn't surprised when Stark didn't offer to pay for her bottle of water and was shocked at what she heard him say to the man standing beside him.

"God damn bitch. She thought she knew what club I should use. Who does she think she is, Nancy Lopez?"

Leigh recognized the name of the LPGA Hall of Fame inductee who had won forty-eight tournaments and several majors during her thirty years on the tour.

"No. That's not right," Stark said with a smirk. "Lopez wasn't a dyke. This chick is." The men around him snickered.

Leigh's bottle of water slipped out of her hand and hit the ground with a thud. Water splashed on her shoes and Stark's right pant leg.

"What the hell?" Stark turned around as quickly as his big body could.

Leigh was still more than a little stunned with the vulgarity that had spewed out of her coworker's mouth. It was one thing for him to think like that, but to say it front of a crowd of complete strangers? What an idiot.

"I'm sorry," she said, all eyes on her. "It just slipped out of my hand."

Peyton came out of nowhere, stepped forward, and picked up her bottle. She gave some cash to the beverage attendant and handed her a fresh bottle of water. The tension in the air was thick. The men who had been chuckling a moment ago suddenly had nothing to say and didn't find things quite so funny anymore. At least they had the good sense to turn away like they'd been caught doing something wrong, which they definitely had.

"Come on, Mike. Let's go. We're up next," one of the men said, smacking his buddy on the arm. They jumped at the opportunity to leave a suddenly very awkward situation.

"Here you go, Mr. Stark." The beverage attendant with a Copperwind name tag that read Heidi sitting prominently on top of her left breast handed Stark a red Solo cup. "Scotch and water, heavy on the scotch, light on the water, and no ice."

Stark looked at Peyton, then fumbled in his pocket and pulled out some cash. *Was that asshole going to make Peyton pay for his drink?*

"So, Leigh," Stark said. "How is that project going, the one your group is working on?"

It was a weak attempt to change the subject, and before Leigh had a chance to tell him so, he quickly said, "I'm going over to talk with the State Farm guy and see if he can get me a discount on my car insurance." It was a feeble excuse and he slithered away.

"Must be a challenge working with him," Peyton said through clenched teeth.

"I don't, at least not very much, thank God."

"Were you aware of his..." Peyton put both palms up as if asking Leigh to finish the sentence for her.

"Chauvinistic, homophobic attitude?" Leigh asked, frowning and shaking her head in disgust. "Yes to the former, no to the latter. I shouldn't be surprised. They usually go together."

"Like scotch and water?"

"Like assholes and bullshit," Leigh replied with as much distaste in her voice as if she were spitting out both. She reached in her pocket and pulled out a five-dollar bill, fully intending to hand it to Peyton, who put her hand up. "No, take it, please. Unlike some people, I don't expect you to buy my drinks."

"It's a bottle of water, and it's my pleasure."

Peyton stepped away before Leigh could say anything else, but she didn't know what that anything else would have been. She was sick to her stomach, a wave of nausea hitting her, so powerful she looked around for a place to toss her breakfast in private. The nausea disappeared as quickly as it came, as well as the opportunity to apologize to Peyton.

Peyton was furious, fuming so much she had to concentrate on her breathing instead of throwing a right hook to the jowls of that asshole Stark. It would definitely be a sucker punch. The fat old man couldn't defend his way out of a speeding ticket, let alone against someone who'd spent nine years in a maximum-security penitentiary.

And then there was Leigh. Stark's comment had obviously surprised her. Her body had stiffened, she'd lost all color in her face, and her bottle of water had slid out of her hand. Peyton had seen red in front of her when she heard his comment and had stepped forward fully intending to do something that would probably cost her her job, if not more. But as soon as she stepped close to Leigh, her anger had subsided, and she was more concerned with Leigh instead of her desire to pummel this ignorant asshole.

Finally, it was Leigh's turn on the tee, and she hit her first shot out of bounds. Her second and third were equally bad, and she three-putted before they mercifully moved to the next hole.

The next two holes were repeats of the one before, and by the time they arrived at the sixteenth tee box, the State Farm guys were bored, Stark had started making snide comments three strokes earlier, and Leigh was a mess.

Peyton knew immediately what had caused Leigh's downward spiral, but it wasn't her place to say anything, and Leigh hadn't asked. As it was, she had to stand on the proverbial sidelines and watch Leigh's game, and her confidence, fall apart. The eighteenth hole couldn't come soon enough, for all of them.

Peyton set Stark's clubs in the designated area by the front door, where the valet would load them into his car after bringing it around. He'd tried to tip her but she'd refused, making up a story about club policy, when in fact, she wanted nothing to do with him or his stinky money. She kept her eye out for Leigh the rest of the afternoon but didn't see her until it was almost time to start the dinner and awards. She was headed out the side door toward the self-service parking lot, and Peyton ran to catch up.

"Leigh. Leigh," she repeated when Leigh didn't acknowledge her. "Leigh, wait." Peyton ran the last few steps. She finally caught up with her next to a red Audi. The lights blinked and the horn honked as she unlocked the doors, so it was obviously Leigh's.

"Are you okay?" She wasn't expecting Leigh to spin around so quickly or for the pain on her face to be so visible.

"Okay? Am I okay? Of course I'm not okay. I embarrassed myself in front of a senior leader in my company, one who has a direct line to the CEO, and you ask if I'm okay?"

"I...uh...it wasn't that bad."

"Wasn't that bad?" Leigh jumped in. "Do you have any idea what this means?"

"No."

"If Stark talks about this afternoon, and believe me, he will, I'll be the laughing stock of the company. Shit!"

"You're kidding, right?" Peyton asked. How could a bad round of golf be as life-altering as Leigh was making it?

What was life-altering had been the last ten years of her life. Peyton had prepared herself for prison as best as she could, watching endless documentaries of life behind locked doors, thick walls, bars, and razor wire. Most were informative, and some scared the holy shit out of her, but she needed to do it. Watching them was like looking at a train wreck. She knew she should stop because she was making herself crazy, but she needed to know as much about her next fifteen years as she could. She was going to a place she never thought she would, even in her worst nightmares. There she'd no longer be Peyton Broader but Inmate #78562.

But Peyton couldn't prepare herself for the emotional impact of being in prison. It consisted of a series of endless routines. Every day was the same as the day before. Up at seven, followed by breakfast, cleaning, and showering. Cells were inspected for damage, and mandatory inmate counts occurred ten times a day. Once a week she could attend a parenting class, an anger-management session, or tutoring for inmates completing their high school degree. There were AA, NA, and prayer meetings every day. Inmates spent most of their time in the day room watching TV, playing cards, or reading outdated magazines brought in by visitors or guards. The only thing that separated Sunday from Tuesday was the nondenominational church services in the morning and visiting day in the afternoon.

No words could describe what it felt like to lose her freedom. Peyton quickly realized she could make herself crazy wondering what her family and friends were doing without her. Did they think about her as much as she thought about them, or did they go on with their lives as if she were just away at school or someplace equally temporary? Did she matter to them less and less every day she was locked up in a cage like an animal?

Before she went to prison, Peyton had been a pre-med student, and somehow, between her classes, golf practice, and her part-time job at Vans Golf Shop, she had managed to get her Emergency Medical Technician certificate. Inmates were given jobs, and Peyton was assigned to the infirmary.

Day in and day out she treated cuts and scrapes, dispensed aspirin for headaches, ibuprofen for cramps, and handed out the never-ending array of pharmaceuticals prescribed for depression, anxiety, and a variety of mental illnesses. The prison psychiatrist did his best to help the women, but the long-term effects of physical, mental, and substance abuse, lack of education, and God knew what else the women had experienced in their history often won the war. And then there were the all-too-frequent effects of prison violence. A physician came into Nelson three times a week for the more serious cases.

For that work, Peyton received a whopping twenty-eight cents an hour, which went directly into her commissary account, and by the time she was released from Nelson she had seventy-two dollars and fifty-five cents. She was issued the amount in cash as well as the clothes she had arrived in before she was escorted out the front door.

Peyton shook her head to rid her mind of those thoughts. It was no good to compare then to now or her life to anyone else's. Everything is relative. Leigh was looking at her like she'd lost her mind by asking the question.

"No. I'm not kidding. Never mind." Leigh tossed her golf bag into her trunk and shut it. The slamming of the driver's door was equally loud.

Chapter Eight

S o, how are things?" Lori asked after the waiter took their drink order and left. Lori had remained her friend during the long ordeal while Peyton's attorney was negotiating her plea and her years inside. Lori wrote to her every week, keeping her up to date on the happenings of the world and often enclosing comic strips from her home-town paper or a copy of a crossword puzzle. Peyton had written to Lori after the first letter arrived, telling her to forget about her and get on with her life. But every time a letter arrived it reminded her that Lori didn't listen.

Peyton hated that question. She had the choice of saying that everything was fine or that she was doing all right. She could also say that the job was good, she'd met some interesting people and some assholes, but for the most part it was okay.

Lori was her only remaining friend from what Peyton referred to as BN, before Nelson. She and Lori had been on the golf team when they won the NCAA Championship her freshman, sophomore, junior, and senior years. Her last year they beat Washington, the year before that, Stanford.

The tournament consisted of four rounds of eighteen holes over the course of four days. It was a team event, low score at the end of the seventy-two holes, and the player with the lowest individual score also received a trophy for winning the entire event

Lori had stuck by Peyton, attending every hearing, visiting her in jail when it was allowed, and making the three-hour trip on the weekends her parents didn't. In the intervening years she'd married Kyle, a pharmacist, and they had two kids, but Lori still made time to see Peyton.

Lori was standing beside her parents the day she was released. She helped her get acclimated back into society but without the overprotectiveness of her parents. One of the terms of her parole was that she couldn't enter any establishment that served liquor unless it sold food as well for a period of twelve months. Lori had hosted several parties and dragged Peyton to those where she had been invited to help Peyton meet new friends and occasionally get laid.

"I have news you might be interested in. Actually, I think you might gloat over it."

Peyton didn't like gossip. It had been rampant at Nelson and was nothing but trouble. Unrest was always brewing, either from the guards or the inmates. Peyton tried to ignore it, keep her nose clean, and stay out of it.

"You know I'm not into gossip."

"This isn't gossip. This is fact. It's about Jolene."

The name of Peyton's former girlfriend used to cause her crippling pain, then rages of anger. Now, all she felt was disgust as to how she could have become involved with someone so shallow.

It was a Sunday, and Peyton waited to be called to the visitors' center. Her parents were always the first to arrive when visiting hours began at one, and they spoke with her for a few minutes before handing the phone to Jolene. This had been the routine every week since Peyton was incarcerated at Nelson four months earlier. Her mother always brought news of her siblings and extended family, while her father sat quietly beside her. Before entering Nelson, Peyton had made it clear she did not want to see anyone in her family while she was there. She wanted to spare them the pain of seeing her in the surroundings she knew would be dreary, depressing, and miserable. But she'd lost the argument with her parents when they explained if they didn't see her, they'd be sick with worry.

They sent photos and cards and well wishes, and Peyton read them, then placed them in the trash. They were heartbreaking

*reminders of what she was missing, and she needed to detach herself
from any thoughts of outside. She needed to focus on where she was,
not where she wasn't. As a result, her side of the two-woman cell
was bare. Nothing adorned her walls. No picture frames sat on the
shelf, nothing that gave any indication she had anyone or anything
on the outside. She did, however, check books out of the library and
had read dozens, catching up on all the fiction she'd missed while
she'd buried her nose in textbooks and played golf every day.*

*It was the third Sunday in her fifth month at Nelson when her
girlfriend Jolene had failed to arrive. She and Jolene had met when
they were sophomores in college and Peyton answered Jolene's ad
for a chemistry tutor. Sparks flew immediately, and despite Jolene's
persistence, Peyton never allowed anything to happen between them
until after her tutoring duties were over. The evening after Jolene's
final, they skipped dinner and went directly to dessert. They'd been
inseparable for the next two years.*

*Jolene was pre-law to Peyton's pre-med, and they would lie
awake after making love and talk about what their life would be like
after they finished their education. Jolene had become withdrawn and
distant the week before Peyton was scheduled to report to Nelson.
Peyton knew it would be difficult for Jolene while she was gone and
had gone so far as to tell Jolene it would be best for them to end their
relationship. Jolene, however, had continued to declare her love for
Peyton and insisted she'd wait for her. But today she didn't come.*

*Peyton glanced at the large, plain, institutional clock high on
the wall in the visitors' room for the third time. It was ten minutes
after one, and Jolene was always there promptly when visiting hours
began. Her parents noticed her clock-watching.*

"She might have got hung up in traffic," her mother offered.

*"Or maybe something came up in one of her cases." That was
her father's attempt at a justification as to Jolene's no-show status.*

*Jolene was a first-year associate at Barker and Hayes, one
of the premier law firms in town. Jolene had told Peyton that as
a rookie, she was expected to produce, at a minimum, sixty hours
of client-billable hours per week. Last week she'd looked tired but
excited as she talked about her cases and the people at the firm.*

Peyton didn't believe either parent, and as the weeks turned into months, not only did Jolene not visit, but she stopped writing, the message clear. Hurt, but realistic enough to realize that Jolene wouldn't wait fifteen years for her, Peyton logged Jolene as another casualty of her actions.

"Your girl find available pussy?"

Peyton kept walking, not acknowledging the disgusting question from Ruth, the resident gossip on B-wing. Nothing was a secret in Nelson. Nothing was private either. Everyone knew who came to visit and who didn't, and when Jolene had stopped coming, everyone in the wing knew it. A few of the women offered their sympathy, while several others tried to muscle their way into her cot. Peyton wasn't interested in having a prison wife before Jolene dumped her, and she wouldn't be anyone's bitch afterward. She'd spent sixty days in solitary when one woman wouldn't take no for an answer and ninety for the same offense a month later.

"She was disbarred, convicted of insider trading," Lori said, tugging Peyton back across memory lane.

Peyton was surprised. She hadn't known what Lori would say about her ex, but it certainly wasn't this.

"Hmm," Peyton said, noncommittal.

"Yeah. I guess she got caught with more than just her hand in the cookie jar. She was sentenced to eighteen months in some federal facility in Texas."

Peyton wasn't sure how she felt. She'd loved Jolene at one time, wanted to marry her, raise a family with her. Now she didn't know if she felt sympathy or pity for the life Jolene was about to have being locked up 24/7. Jolene would experience every possible indignity and be stripped of humanity. Peyton had a lingering desire for Jolene to experience the pain she had felt when she dumped her.

"I read about it in the paper," Lori said, dumping three packets of sweetener into her iced tea. "After I heard, I googled the story, and it had her mug shot. God, Peyton, she looked like she was facing her executioner. I know you don't care about her anymore, but karma's a bitch, isn't it?"

"I feel nothing for her."

"I know, but I just can't help but smile when I think about it. The way she treated you." Lori would often make her opinion of Jolene known. There was no doubt what she thought of her.

"Lori, I don't want to talk about it, and I don't want to talk about her."

Lori knew that tone and changed the subject. "So, have you met any interesting people at the club?"

Instantly, Leigh's face popped into her head. "Everybody's interesting in their own way."

Lori chastised her. "That's not what I mean, and you know it."

"Lori, you know I don't do that."

"I know. I'm just worried about you."

"Well, don't be. I'm fine."

"Peyton, I'm no expert on this subject, although I will admit I read everything I could get my hands on about individuals released from prison, and you are not all right." Lori used her fingers to make air quotes around the last two words. "You haven't been out that long. You're still getting acclimated to going where you want, when you want, meeting people, meeting women." Lori had stayed with Peyton in her apartment for the first week, helping her adjust.

"And that works out fine until they start asking deeper, probing questions. What do you do, how long have you done it, what did you do before, where did you go to school, how did you get that scar?"

"What do you say?"

"Nothing. I make some vague reference to something, then change the subject."

"I know—"

"No, Lori. You don't." Peyton suddenly felt guilty at the look of hurt that flashed over her best friend's face. "I'm sorry. I didn't mean that. You don't know what it's like. Don't you remember what it was like when I was arrested? It was a feeding frenzy. My parents couldn't leave their house, and the fucking media sharks and protestors on both sides trampled their yard and invaded their privacy. Their neighbors were furious at them. In fact, some of them still are. And they had to relive it when I got out. My name, my face is out there. Most people don't recognize me, but I know when somebody does or when they can't quite place where they've seen me before.

"I was trying to hook up with this one woman. I don't even remember what her name was. She kept pestering me about it, and, like an idiot, I told her. Then she wanted to know every detail. Was it like the Netflix show *Orange is the New Black?* Was it like the old HBO series *Oz?* Did people shank each other, get raped in the shower? Did I ever have to kill anyone inside? I swear, the more questions she asked, the hotter she got. I finally just fucked her and left. That's what she wanted anyway. Now I'm sure she tells all her friends that she slept with a murderer, which makes her the bad girl. What she should feel is ashamed."

"Come on, Peyton. Why do you say that?"

"I am. I'm a murderer."

"No, you're not." Lori's voice was hard and firm with emphasis. "You are Peyton Broader, three-time NCAA Golfer of the year and the two-time NCAA athlete of the year, college graduate with a degree in one of the toughest fields there is. You are a daughter, sister, and a fabulous best friend. You killed someone who deserved to be killed. That doesn't make you a murderer. You are still you. I don't ever want to hear you say that again. I can't control what you think, but that's not what I see in front of me. I see a strong woman who did the right thing and has survived the adversity that came with it. Don't let it turn you into something you're not. I won't let you."

CHAPTER NINE

"Peyton and NCAA and collegiate golf," Leigh said as her fingers flew across the keyboard. It was Monday morning, and she'd almost gone back to bed to start the day over. She'd overslept after hours of nightmares that included Stark laughing at her with his hyena laugh and Peyton knocking the slimeball on his ass when he continued his homophobic comments about her. She knew her eyes were puffy, and she got to work so late she'd had to park at the end of the lot. Thankfully she didn't have any meetings this morning.

Stark had probably told everyone about her collapse on the course because several people had walked by and looked into her office with more curiosity than they ever had. Obviously, the word was out, thank you very much, Peter Prick.

Her office was twenty feet by twenty-five, the city skyline filling the bank of windows behind her desk. An equal number was directly in front of her as well, giving the entire area an airy, open feel but creating privacy in her office.

Her curiosity about Peyton finally got the best of her, and Google could turn up anything if you typed in the right string of keywords. She didn't know Peyton's last name, but she was sure she'd played golf in college and, based on how well she played with them, had been pretty damn good.

Over four thousand hits come up with a variety of headings, the second one catching her eye. PEYTON BROADER, REPEATS AS NCAA

GOLFER OF THE YEAR. She clicked on the hyperlink, and it took her directly to an article that talked about Peyton's golf career at Louisiana State University. Peyton had entered LSU as a freshman at seventeen with a full-ride golf scholarship.

Leigh read about Peyton's achievements on the golf links and, due to her winning the NCAA Golfer of the Year, how she had an automatic exemption to play on the LPGA tour. She finished in the top ten in every tournament she played but was unable to accept any prize money, which would have negated her scholarship eligibility.

"I'm focused on finishing my education, then going on to medical school, not dropping out to play on the tour," Peyton was quoted as saying at the Women's U.S. Open her first year. Given her scholastic experience, Peyton had been on track to do just that. She'd graduated summa cum laude with a dual major in physics and biochemistry. She'd been accepted to several of the most prestigious medical schools in the country but had chosen to stay close to home and attend the University of Arizona.

Leigh was just about to read the next article when her boss knocked on her door and she waved him in.

"How was the tournament," Larry asked, innocently.

Larry Taylor, their CEO and her boss, was six feet nine inches tall and a marathon runner who proudly displayed the finisher medals of his races on a wall in his office. He was also more than a weekend golfer. He didn't look the part of the executive of a multibillion-dollar company who spent more time in boardrooms than outside. Leigh had read in the annual report that he was sixty-two, married to his college sweetheart, and had four kids. He valued teamwork, camaraderie, and work-life balance. He played golf every Saturday, and in the summer, when the sun set later, he played two or three times a week.

Leigh had heard through the rumor mill that Larry took his golf clubs and running shoes on every business trip, often making time for both sports.

"It was great," she replied honestly. "It was a beautiful day, beautiful venue, great course." Other than her complete humiliation in front of Peyton and Stark, she'd had a wonderful time.

"Peter said you had a little trouble on the back nine."

"Well, we all have one of those rounds we just want to simply forget," Leigh said, the line she'd rehearsed all day yesterday.

Larry looked at her so intently Leigh started to get nervous

"Are you okay, Leigh?" he asked, concern on his face as well as in his voice.

"Of course. Why wouldn't I be?"

"I don't know." He stared at her so intensely again that Leigh wanted to look away. "Out of sorts, I guess," he added.

Leigh tried to laugh it off, but it came out more of a *hrmph* instead. "My sorts are fine. I appreciate your concern, Larry."

Larry strolled around her office, picking up a framed photo of her standing proud at the finish line of a motocross race, her teammates flanking her.

"You race?" Larry asked with more than a little curiosity.

"Yes. I do. Those are the guys I ride with."

"That's one sport I've never tried. The idea of driving fifty miles an hour on dirt roads with the only thing between you and a major road rash a small motorcycle makes me shudder." And Larry did just that.

"We have protective gear." Leigh pointed to the helmet, chest protector, elbow and knee pads, and the specially made knee-high boots to protect her ankles from snapping if they hit the ground the wrong way.

"I see that, but too much risk for me," he said. "My wife would kill me if I picked up another sport." He changed the subject. "We're still on to play when I get back from overseas, right?"

"Yes, we are," Leigh answered. "I'm looking forward to it," Leigh lied.

"As am I," Larry said. "I'd like to get to know you better, your family, what else you do in your spare time, that sort of thing."

Leigh wondered what Larry would do if he found out she dated women and was a better motocross rider than golfer.

"I'm sorry it couldn't be sooner, schedules being what they are and my three weeks of traveling to our other locations."

"I understand. It gives me a chance to polish my game a little."

"You'll be fine," Larry said, and looked at his watch. "Oh, gotta run. I'll see you when I get back."

"Yes, sir. You too. Safe travels."

When Larry left, she just sat down in her chair, swiveled it to look out the window, and placed her feet on the credenza that paralleled her desk. Her cell phone rang, and as she fished it out of her briefcase she saw that it was Rick Henderson, the president of her motocross club. She'd met Rick years ago while riding her dirt bike on a trail surrounding Lake Pleasant, forty-five minutes from her house. She'd just finished a grueling trail and was guzzling a cherry Gatorade when he pulled up next to her.

"Hi. I'm Rick Henderson. I've seen you out here before."

Leigh was hot, tired, and more than a little grungy, in no mood to deflect the clueless advances of some straight guy, so she didn't say anything.

"I have a club, just a bunch of us that get together and ride and do a few races here and there, and we're always looking for good riders."

Leigh still didn't say anything. Good-looking riders, she thought.

"Here." Rick dug in his pocket and pulled out his wallet. "This is us, The Desperados," he said, handing Leigh a business card. "I know it's a ridiculous name, but we're just a bunch of guys that are probably having a midlife crisis."

Leigh looked at the card and saw a cool-looking logo, a website address, and information on a Facebook page.

"Check us out," he said, nodding toward the card in Leigh's hand. She still hadn't said anything. Rick squirmed in his seat, his bright-red helmet in his lap.

"Look. I'm not coming on to you. I'm happily married with three kids and a wife who lets me ride around with a bunch of guys on Saturdays."

"What would she say if it were a bunch of guys and a woman?"

"She'd probably say it's about time we added some diversity to our club. Other than Michael," he added. "He's African American."

"Well, she doesn't have to worry about me taking her husband. I'm not into husbands, or any male for that matter." Leigh didn't normally come out to everyone she met, but for some reason she liked Rick and was interested in finding out more about his club.

"Even better," Rick said, nonplussed. *"My daughter's a lesbian. Jenny Henderson. You know her?"*

Leigh couldn't help but laugh at Rick. He was so sincere. *"We don't all know each other, Rick."*

He flushed with embarrassment. *"Sorry about that. Jenny says I can be really stupid sometimes."* He kicked the dirt with his black riding boot. *"Think about it. We're out here every Saturday except the first one of the month. We make camp and gear up over there,"* he pointed over his shoulder to his left, *"at eight. Our wives come with, sometimes our kids, and we ride most of the morning, then grab a bite at the camp before we head home. We really are harmless, and, well, we need a sixth for our team. Tom transferred to Chicago, and we've been short for several months. We've missed a few races because of it."*

Leigh had visited the website for Desperados and their Facebook page. From what she could tell, they were exactly what Rick had said they were—a bunch of middle-aged men riding motocross bikes. She'd called him later that week and had been riding with them for the past three years.

She answered the phone, grateful for something to take her mind off the last few minutes.

Chapter Ten

U gh! I've got to take some lessons," Leigh said, propping her golf bag next to several others in the corner of the room.

"What's wrong?" Jill asked. "You played for shit all day."

"I don't know. It's probably PTSD after playing that round with Stark." Leigh had told Jill of her breakdown on the last seven holes. "I'm traumatized." Leigh tried to laugh it off, but it really bothered her.

"What are you going to do?" Jill asked as they walked to the bar and sat on the tall stools.

"I guess I'll call around and try to get some lessons."

"How about Peyton?" Jill said as if it were a foregone conclusion.

"Peyton?" Leigh said, her heart jumping and her stomach fluttering at the attractive golf pro's name. Based on her reaction to Peyton's name and every time she thought of her and the very, very vivid dream of her last night, Leigh wasn't sure she'd be able to pay attention to what Peyton was trying to teach her. Her eyes were piercing and looked like she didn't miss a thing.

"I Googled her the other day." Leigh hadn't intended to tell anyone, but Jill was her best friend and a sound ear.

Jill leaned forward, her forearms on the table "What did you find out?" Jill evidently sensed something so Leigh needed to be careful.

"She's pretty good, or at least she was." Leigh recited the facts she'd learned about Peyton.

"She'd be perfect. She's seen you play a couple of times and probably already knows what you need to fix. Call her, right now. Better yet, go over to the clubhouse and sign up."

"I am not going over to the clubhouse, and I don't need to call her right now."

"Yes, you do. You'll overthink it and talk yourself out of it."

Jill knew her too well.

"Do you have any idea how expensive this is going to be?"

"Leigh, you make at least a couple hundred thousand dollars a year, and Peyton's going to charge, what, one hundred, two hundred dollars an hour? Don't you think that's a good investment to save you the embarrassment of another meltdown, this time in front of your boss? This might be the biggest game of your life. How can you afford not to? Now, tell me the last time you had sex."

Leigh almost choked on her beer. "What?"

"Sex, you know, that thing that feels really good, and even better when you do it with someone?" Jill loved sex. She loved talking about it, getting it, and was one of the few women who could say clitoris and orgasm as easy as she said peanut butter and jelly. To Jill, sex was as normal and important to life as breathing.

"I am so not telling you the last time I had sex," Leigh said but knew she'd end up doing just that.

"That long, huh?"

"Jill." Leigh's voice betrayed just how tired she was of this conversation.

"I'm going to continue to hound you because it seems like the only time you actually have sex is when I badger you into it."

"So now you're saying the only time I have sex is when you tell me to?"

"Isn't that what happened with Stephanie and what was her name? Indy or something?"

"Her name was Indiana."

"Jeez. Does that mean her parents conceived her in Indiana or was she born there?"

"I didn't ask."

"My point exactly."

"What are you talking about?" Leigh asked sharply, tired of this subject.

"You're never with someone long enough to find out about her."

"Weren't you the one who told me the other day to go out and hook up and have wild sex?"

Yes, I did because you're really uptight, Leigh. I know," Jill said, holding her hands up in defense. "You told me after you got this job, blah, blah, blah. Well, let me tell you, Leigh. Your life has gotten crazier. More pressure, more visibility, less fun time."

"And I'm supposed to…what? Stock up on sex now?"

"Hmm," Jill said, pursing her lips and frowning. "I never thought about it in that way. But that won't work."

"Why not?"

"Because the more you have it, the more you want it."

Leigh rolled her eyes, shook her head, and playfully kicked Jill under the table. "Fine. I'll get laid."

CHAPTER ELEVEN

Peyton pulled into the strip mall and parked in the only space available. Busy day at the parole office, she thought, putting her truck in park and gathering her paperwork. One of the conditions of Peyton's early release was that she had to check in with her parole officer twice a week for the first six months, then weekly thereafter.

Manny Conway was a fifty-nine-year-old overworked, overweight, twenty-eight-year veteran of the Department of Corrections Parole Enforcement Division. According to Conway, he didn't take bullshit from anyone, and he could see right through it as well. He made it clear that he thought Peyton got a sweet deal with her early release, and he planned to keep a very close eye on her.

Conway expected his parolees to abide by the rules, one of which was that he had the right to inspect their place of residence as well as their place of business any time of the day or night. In the first three weeks, he'd shown up at her house nine times and at Copperwind eight. Each time Peyton invited him in, having nothing to hide from the man who controlled if, and when, she returned to Nelson to finish her entire sentence.

Unlike many other criminals who had been released, she had a family who loved her, would look out for her, and give her a place to live and a job. The reason she was in Nelson in the first place, and the likelihood that she would repeat her crime, no longer existed.

Peyton hated how the news media always referred to Chandler as the *alleged* suspect. He'd done it, no doubt about it. The two detectives arresting her, Ruth Smallsreed and Joanne Hiller, broke protocol and told her that the video he had stupidly made very clearly showed his face as well as Lizzy's. That, and the fact that Lizzy had picked him out in a lineup and had described a unique birthmark on Chandler was enough evidence for Peyton that *alleged* was no longer applicable.

She had to slam the door of her truck; otherwise it wouldn't close properly. It was, after all, thirty-four years old and a similar make and model to the one she had painstakingly restored before Nelson. She'd told her father to sell it to pay for her mounting legal fees, and as much as it broke her heart, she'd never looked back. That would only cause pain.

She pulled open the door going into the office, the handle hot due to its western exposure. She welcomed the blast of cool air as she stepped inside.

"Hello, Peyton," Roseanne, the fifty-something-year-old clerk at the registration desk, said. "On time, as usual." Roseanne made a note on her pad while Peyton signed in on a spiral-bound book on the counter. "I wish all of our clients were as punctual as you." Roseanne's voice was muffled, having to pass through a two-inch bullet-proof window.

"Good afternoon, Roseanne. How are you?"

"I'm good."

It had taken Roseanne a while to warm up to her. Peyton was sure the woman had seen a load of bullshit from the people coming in the door and didn't believe anything they said. Peyton had made it a point to be on time, if not early, for every appointment, her paperwork completed neatly and legibly, and always the best dressed in the waiting area.

"How is Jerry doing?" Peyton asked, referring to Roseanne's son, a freshman at the University of Florida.

"His grades started to tank, and I had to have a come-to-Jesus with the boy. I think he's back on the right track."

"And I'm sure he'll stay there," Peyton added, sliding her papers in the slot under the window. Roseanne had stopped checking them for completeness after her fourth appointment. Now she simply stamped them as Peyton sat down in one of the black vinyl chairs in the waiting area.

She'd brought a book to read, not only because she was early but because Conway always ran behind. It was just a petty power thing. A large, light-skinned man beside Peyton coughed several times, his girth overfilling the arms of the chair and rubbing against Peyton's hip when he moved. He covered his mouth with his hands, then wiped them on the thighs of his pants. Peyton didn't touch anything in this room or anywhere in the building, for that matter, for just this reason. Not only did she have to worry about catching a cough or a cold, like everyone else, but tuberculosis and a variety of other communicable diseases were probably growing on every surface. Every time she got back to her truck she squirted enough hand sanitizer on her hands to kill the bubonic plague. When she returned home she scrubbed them in her bathroom sink, using the strongest antibacterial soap she could get her hands on.

She'd become a bit OCD about germs while in Nelson, and with as much spittle, blood, and other bodily fluids everywhere, she had every right. However, in Nelson she could do very little about it except wash her hands with the overpriced soap she bought in the commissary.

Some of the guards would fuck with her when they came into her cell for inspection or just to be assholes. They'd cough when they picked up her books and thumbed through the pages. They'd sneeze when they inspected her pillow for contraband and carry out a variety of other equally disgusting actions they used to get under her skin. None of them worked, as Peyton was determined to get out of Nelson as soon as she could, and that meant no issues with the guards.

The prisoners had a certain hierarchy. The bottom of the food chain consisted of those that hurt kids, the top reserved for those who killed the people who hurt the kids. Obviously, Peyton had been at the top of that food chain, which garnered her some level of respect from her fellow inmates and downright hatred from others. Actual money rarely meant anything. Drugs, sex, and power were the currency in every prison in America, and Nelson was no exception.

A man across the room was having a conversation with himself, the woman beside him wiping her nose with the back of her hand. Her leg was bouncing up and down rhythmically. She'd probably tried to clean herself up so she could pass the mandatory drug test, but if her parole officer was as astute as Conway, it wouldn't matter.

One by one her fellow parolees disappeared behind the combination-locked, scuffed brown door until finally her name was called. She followed a man down a hallway of offices, each with clear glass as walls. She hadn't been told, but she'd figured out that the décor was not for aesthetics but to enable the other parole officers to keep an eye on any trouble that might be brewing with their peers. She stopped at the entrance to Conway's office. She never entered until he told her to.

"Have a seat, Broader," Conway said, tossing a yellow folder across his desk. His overworked chair groaned in protest. "What have you been up to?" he asked, not looking at her folder the other man handed him.

"Working. We're starting to pick up at the club, and I'm keeping busy."

"What are you doing?"

Conway was an ass, pure and simple. He had made it clear early on that he'd been on the side that held up the signs that advocated throwing away the key when Peyton was locked up. Peyton kept her patience as he repeated the same question he asked every time she sat across from him. In addition to his obvious conflict of interest in her case, he wasn't the sharpest knife in the drawer.

"I work six days a week, maybe seven, if they need me. I caddie or fill in if another golfer is needed, work in the pro shop. A little bit of everything."

Conway opened the green folder in front of him, the one with her full name written in bold, black letters across the top.

"Let's see now," he said, moving a few pieces of paper around like it was the first time he'd ever seen them. He gave a cursory glance at the papers inside, having to know what he'd see. Peyton sat across from him. She had brought copies of her pay stubs, rent receipts, utility bills, all showing she was gainfully employed and had a place to live.

"You work at your brother's golf course. The fancy one up north."

"Yes, I do. Copperwind," Peyton said, just as she had every other time he'd asked.

"You pay your rent on time, or so says the same brother that gave you a job," Conway said with disdain.

Peyton had never been able to figure out why Conway was so antagonistic toward her. Sure, she was released early, but so was everybody else in the over-packed, smelly waiting room down the hall.

"Yes. I rent the room over his garage."

"How convenient."

"I'm lucky to have a supportive family, a good job, and a stable roof over my head. They want me to put my time at Nelson behind me and be successful."

"I'll determine if your time at Nelson is behind you, not them." He practically snarled. "Do you have a girlfriend?" he asked with a sneer.

"No."

"Why not? Nobody want to sleep with a murderer? They probably have every reason to be afraid you'll shoot them in the head in the afterglow."

"Mr. Conway, the reason I was in Nelson will never happen again. I'm not a habitual criminal, a drug addict, or a thief."

"But you are a murderer."

Peyton inhaled and let her breath out slowly, keeping in mind what Jill had told her the other night. "I killed Norman Chandler because he kidnapped and raped my sister."

"Allegedly." Conway quickly corrected her. "He hadn't even gone to trial, let alone been convicted."

"As I said, the reason I was in Nelson will never happen again. I don't date because I'm focusing on my job and getting my life back." And it's none of your fucking business, she thought.

Conway looked at her with hard, untrusting eyes. "Yes, Broader, you do have it better than ninety-nine percent of my clients. But don't think that will get you any special treatment. No sireee. Not from me."

This was the same speech she heard from him every time she came in. It was old and tiring and simply bullshit.

"No. I don't think that. I never have, and you've proved that as well." Peyton couldn't help adding a little jab. Conway wasn't sharp enough to pick it up.

"Well, I don't believe you, Broader." He closed the folder and looked at the information printed on the front and made a short note. "You have five more months," he said, referring to the time left on her parole, after which she would be released from its terms and conditions.

"Yes, I do." Peyton knew to the day when she would no longer be under the controlling thumb of this man.

Conway glared at her for a long time. Peyton had gotten pretty good at reading people, but she couldn't read him. Conway wanted her to squirm, people who craved power usually did, but she'd done nothing wrong, had nothing to be guilty about. She sat there quietly.

Finally, he said, "Get out of here. Be sure to make your appointment with Roseanne on the way out." He put her folder on the stack on the corner of his desk and pulled another from the pile on his right.

"Thank you. Have a good day."

Ten minutes later, Peyton was back in her truck and driving down the highway, her next appointment written on the business-card-size paper in her wallet.

Her mind wandered as she maneuvered the stop-and-go heavy traffic on the interstate. It had gotten easier to switch from parolee to citizen each subsequent time she left Conway's office. The reference to the time remaining on her parole made her think about her first parole hearing.

It was five years into her sentence, and Peyton was nervous. She'd researched the proceedings and politely tolerated the unsolicited advice from several of the women who had gone through them. She didn't listen to them because—duh—they were still inside. One woman told her to confess her sins, beg for forgiveness, say she'd found Jesus and would forever live a life in his name. Peyton had already confessed, would never beg for forgiveness, and had never lost Jesus. Another told her to lie and say whatever they were looking to hear. Peyton couldn't do that either. She'd known exactly what she was doing at the time and had consciously decided to do it. She refused to minimize that fact just to get out early.

"Ms. Broader, would you please tell us the nature of your conviction?" the man sitting in the middle of the two women and four men asked.

"Voluntary manslaughter." Peyton's voice was surprisingly calm, a complete opposite of her nerves.

"You plead guilty to killing Norman Chandler. Is that correct?"

"Yes."

"Mr. Chandler allegedly molested your sister. Is that correct?" the man asked, thumbing through the folder in front of him.

Peyton didn't believe for a minute that everyone at the table in front of her didn't know the details of her case. At least she hoped the system that determined parolees was effective.

"No sir," Peyton said respectfully. Every head looked up from their paperwork. "Chandler kidnapped her, held her for three days, raped her, beat her unconscious, and broke her jaw, three ribs, and her left arm. She was nine." Molested was too benign to describe what had happened to Lizzy. She saw the women wince and one of the men look away.

"And you shot him?"

"Yes sir, I did." No point in being anything other than direct.

"You took it upon yourself to be judge, jury, and executioner?"

"Yes."

"And you decided to take justice into your own hands?" one of the other men asked, the question repetitive.

"My sister was afraid he would come back for her. She had nightmares and was afraid to be alone or leave the house."

"*So you killed him?*"

"*Yes.*" Only one of the parole members could look her in the eyes. "*If it could give her peace of mind, it was worth it.*" That had been her justification then, and it hadn't changed.

"*If you had the chance to do it all over again, would you?*" one of the women asked.

Peyton didn't hesitate. "*Yes, ma'am. I would.*" She knew that wasn't the answer they were looking for and that she'd just blown her chance to be released early. She didn't care. It was the truth.

CHAPTER TWELVE

"Will you be around after the tournament?"
Peyton had checked in several attractive women for
the LGBT tournament, but this one couldn't keep her eyes to herself.
She was wearing fashionable, very expensive golf attire that, in
Peyton's opinion, was one size too small. This woman, however, was
obviously very aware of how it accentuated her attractive curves.

"I work here, so yes, I will. Enjoy your day." Peyton had gotten
very good at deflecting unwanted attention and managed to do the
same with this one without pissing her off.

"Peyton?"

She looked up from the list of registered attendees. "Hilde.
How are you?"

"Even better now that I know you're here," she said, winking
at Peyton.

"I work here, Hilde, and this is an important day. Everyone's
working."

Hilde leaned over, placing both palms on the table, her face
close to Peyton's. If Peyton wanted to, she could look down the front
of Hilde's top, and Peyton was sure that was the woman's intent.

"Who do I have to pay to get you in my foursome?" she asked
in what she probably thought was a seductive whisper.

"I'm afraid that's not possible." Peyton was growing tired of
everyone hitting on her as if she was one of the prizes. She shuffled
her papers, looking for Hilde's name.

"Is Leigh here?"

Peyton had looked at the registration board several times a day for Leigh's name, and finally, yesterday, it was the last one on the list.

"Not yet." Peyton had been waiting for Leigh to show up since she sat down behind the table an hour ago. She'd kept the line moving, one eye on the next person in anticipation of seeing Leigh. She put an X next to Hilde's name and handed her a participant packet, then signaled for the next person in line to step up.

"Good luck."

Finally, Leigh was standing in front of her, a teasing smile on her face.

"Leigh Marshall, checking in."

"Ms. Marshall, welcome to Copperwind." Peyton played along. She exaggerated marking Leigh's name off the list, then handed her the nylon pouch with the Copperwind logo on the front. Inside was her tournament shirt and several other golf-related goodies. "You're all present and accounted for. This is your participant packet. Inside is your pairing information and some information about the rest of the day. You tee off on the eighth hole for our shotgun start." In a shotgun start, each foursome begins on a different hole. Leigh and her group would begin on the eighth hole and finish their eighteen holes on the seventh. Leigh and Jill were paired with two men from the LGBT Youth Center. Hilde and her foursome were on the sixth. At the end of the eighteen holes, the pairing with the lowest score won the tournament, and the individual with the lowest score won the individual trophy.

"Thank you," Leigh said, peering into her goodie bag. "Are you playing today?"

"Unfortunately, no. It's all hands on deck today, so I'll be doing just about anything Marcus needs me to."

Peyton didn't want Leigh to leave. She'd waited for her to arrive, and within three or four minutes, it was over. She wanted to talk with her but didn't know what about, and the dozen or so people in the line behind Leigh prohibited any further conversation.

"Have a good tournament," Peyton said just before Leigh headed for the locker room.

❖

Peyton wasn't able to catch up with Leigh and her group until the twelfth hole. She watched her for several moments before Leigh saw her, smiled, and waved her over.

"How are we doing?" she asked, indicating her and Jill.

"No coaching from the staff allowed," Peyton said lightly. It was the tournament rule, but she wasn't heavy-handed in telling Leigh so. "My lips are sealed." Peyton mimicked zipping a zipper on her lips, and Leigh's eyes lingered on them so long, Jill jabbed her in the side.

"Earth to Leigh."

"Oh, yeah. Sorry."

Peyton laughed. "It doesn't matter how you play. It's all in good fun and for a worthy cause," Peyton said, very interested in Leigh's reaction. The LGBT Youth Center desperately needed extensive repairs, its eighty-year-old building showing its age.

Peyton chatted up the other members of Leigh and Jill's group enough to be polite, then went on her way. She would have liked to stay longer, but it was their turn to tee off, and she had other things to do. She'd taken a quick detour to see Leigh, and her welcoming smile was well worth it.

Peyton ran into Leigh twice more before the day ended, close to five thirty. By the time dinner was over, the speeches and thanks conveyed, and the awards handed out, it was almost ten. Several players took advantage of the Copperwind free Uber service to get home safely. Peyton saw Jill leave earlier, and when Leigh was ready to go, she walked her out.

"Is free escort service part of the registration fees?" Leigh asked teasingly.

"Absolutely," Peyton replied, her blood warm from Leigh's laughter. "I hope you had a good day."

"Absolutely." Leigh knowingly echoed her. "The weather was perfect, and we had a great group. We didn't golf worth a damn, but we had fun, and that's what was important. That, and the thousand bucks I dropped at the silent auction."

The auction was one of the tournament favorites, with businesses all over town donating goods or services to the cause. It was a tax write-off for the donors and the buyers, a win-win for everyone. A piece of paper and a pen lay next to each item, and the bidders entered their bidder number and amount they were willing to pay. If another bidder wanted to raise the price, they repeated the process until the bidding closed. The name and amount at the bottom of the list won. All the elements of an auction without all the noise.

"What did you win?" Peyton had been outside when the winners of each item were announced. Must be nice to have that much discretionary money to throw around. After the money she gave her parents and Marcus for rent, she barely had enough to cross the street.

"A golf lesson with an instructor of my choice at some swanky golf course called Copperwind," Leigh said as if she'd never heard of the place.

"Really? I heard that was one of the most sought-after items." Peyton had noticed the bidding climb in hundred-dollar increments the few times she passed by the table and remembered seeing the same number every third or fourth line on the sheet.

"I don't know who number eight was, but I wasn't going to let that item get away."

"Well, be sure to cash it in. That's a lot of money to spend if you don't use it."

"Oh, I definitely will," Leigh said. "This is me." She pointed to a bright-red Audi A4 as the lights flashed and the dome light lit up the interior.

Peyton had a case of nerves, as if it were the end of their first date and the will-she, won't-she-kiss-me question was hanging in the air. Of course she wouldn't kiss her. Leigh was a member, and that was a no-no.

"Well, thanks for walking me out. I had a great time," she said, opening the driver's door.

She hesitated, looking in her eyes, then to her lips. Peyton wasn't sure, but all indications were that Leigh was going to kiss her. Instead she simply said good night.

"Good night. Drive safe," Peyton said just before she closed her door.

Peyton watched Leigh drive out of the parking lot, and her red taillights turned onto the main street. What a bizarre ending to an interesting day.

Chapter Thirteen

The pounding on her front door woke Peyton from a fitful sleep. Between dreams of Leigh Marshall and nightmares that her early release was a mistake, she hadn't slept much. She quickly dressed in a pair of jeans and a T-shirt, knowing who was there. She stopped at the desk and pulled out a small tape recorder and turned it on. She hid it behind the clock on the shelf.

After Conway's first midnight visit, Peyton had bought the voice-activated device for her own protection, after he intimated that he was looking for more than compliance to the terms and conditions of her parole. Nelson had taught her how to side-step ugly situations, and she had effectively done so that time and several others as well. She knew there would be a time when she wouldn't be able to. With guys like Conway, there always was.

Manny Conway pushed the door open, slamming it into the wall, his hand on the butt of his gun holstered on his hip. He grabbed Peyton on the shoulder, spun her around, and pushed her up against the open door.

"Who you got with you tonight?"

"Nobody," Peyton said as she gritted her teeth at the indignity of his hands on her. The first time it happened, he said he was searching her for weapons or contraband. She knew that wasn't the case. He was copping a feel, nothing more.

"On your knees, cross your ankles, hands behind your head," he growled, looking around. She knew after he cuffed her that he'd search her apartment. This was the standard welfare check he subjected her to. She didn't struggle or say anything. It would only give him an excuse to revoke her parole.

Peyton fumed as she heard him rummaging around in her bedroom. The last time he was here he'd pulled everything out of her dresser, including the drawer, and from her closet, tossing it all on the floor, where she was left to clean up. It had taken her all day to wash everything she owned. Peyton couldn't stand the thought of putting on clothes his slimy hands had touched. She threw out all her underwear and bought new ones.

She made a mental note to install hidden security cameras in every room so she could document, without a doubt, his inappropriate treatment of her. At least she thought it was inappropriate. What the hell did she know about the roles and responsibilities of a parole officer? She'd assumed they had a job to do, not that they would get off on humiliating their parolees.

"So, you didn't get lucky tonight, Broader?"

Conway might have thought he was going to get an answer to his intrusive question, but no way would she give him the satisfaction. It was none of his fucking business.

"What's the matter, Broader? Cat got your tongue? Or is it pussy? Your girlfriend wear out your tongue?" Conway laughed at his own crude joke.

Peyton clenched her teeth together so tightly she wouldn't be surprised if she didn't break a tooth or two. The balls he had and the way he abused his power disgusted her.

"I asked you a question, Broader. I expect an answer."

"I went to work, came home, fixed some dinner, and watched the ball game. That was the extent of my evening."

"Hmm. You can't tell me a good-looking dyke like you doesn't get lucky every chance she can."

Peyton had gotten lucky, as Conway so crudely described it, every time she'd wanted to. And she wanted it a lot. She kept her affairs brief and noncommittal, and she wouldn't even go so far as to call them affairs. They were mere hookups, both her and the other woman getting exactly what they wanted. She wasn't in the market for any kind of relationship and chose her women for the same attitude.

She'd been celibate for the nine years, two months, and eight days she'd been in Nelson. Three thousand, three hundred, fifty-four nights, give or take two or three leap years. Even though she was surrounded by two thousand women, she wasn't interested in hooking up with anyone. Hooking up meant you cared, and if you cared, people could use that weakness against her. Peyton refused to give anyone anything they could use to their advantage.

Conway trashed her living room, tossing the cushions on her couch before upending it and doing the same to the recliner Marcus had given her just last week. Finally, he stepped behind her, grabbed her cuffed wrists, and yanked her to her feet. Peyton stifled a scream of pain.

Conway stood so close behind her she could feel his stinky breath on the back of her neck, his crotch level with her hands cuffed behind her back. There was no mistaking how much Conway got off on harassing her, and Peyton resisted the urge to grab and squeeze. Finally, her hands were freed, and calmly and slowly she turned to face him, masking the anger in her eyes.

Conway licked his lips as his bloodshot eyes stared at her chest and ended between her legs, making several trips before he finally turned and walked out her front door.

Peyton rushed over and threw the deadbolt before her legs could give out. When they did, she slid to the floor, her back against the door, and wrapped her arms around her legs.

"God damn son of a bitch."

Peyton didn't know how long she sat there, but when the morning sun started to peek through the crack in the drapes in her front window, she got up, went straight to her computer, and ordered a dozen miniature video cameras from Amazon Prime, selecting same-day delivery. The entire system cost only a few hundred bucks, but it almost depleted her emergency money. At least if Conway came again as soon as tonight, she'd be ready for him.

CHAPTER FOURTEEN

"Peyton, are you all right?" Lori asked the next day at lunch. "And don't say you're fine, because I know you better than to believe it."

"Conway dropped in last night."

"Did he do something to you?"

Peyton had shared with her best friend the nocturnal visits of her parole officer, and Lori had threatened to report his behavior to his superiors. Peyton had convinced her otherwise, saying that not only could she take care of herself, but doing so would only increase the likelihood of her parole being revoked for some fictitious reason. Conway was a bully, and Peyton knew how to handle bullies. However, the very real possibility that Conway would revoke her parole for some trumped-up reason scared the ever-living hell out of her. If she needed to take his shit to be free of him, she would.

"No. Or I should say nothing he hadn't already done." It had taken Peyton the better part of the morning to clean up the evidence of his power play, and she still had several loads of laundry to do. She'd thrown away her sheets and had to stop and get another set on the way home.

"I know I've told you this before, but you need to be careful with him, Peyton."

"I ordered some video cameras. They should be arriving sometime this afternoon."

"I'll get a babysitter, and Kyle and I will come over and help you install them."

Lori's husband was an absolute gem. Between him and Marcus, they'd turned the rotting empty space above Marcus's garage into a nice apartment for her.

"And don't tell me you don't need any help. We're coming. You can buy pizza. We'll bring the beer."

True to her word, Lori and her husband showed up at five thirty, the back of Kyle's pickup filled with a ladder, drill, and various other tools he needed to effectively hide the cameras. It took them over an hour to decide on the right place to put each one, ensuring 100 percent coverage of her apartment. It took another hour to install the first one and connect it to the power supply. The second took half as long, and by ten thirty all of them were installed and they'd eaten a large pizza. The cameras were motion-activated, and she could control them with an app on her phone. Lori had programmed it for her and written step-by-step instructions on how to erase the video after Peyton had watched it.

"I asked around about how other parole officers operate," Kyle said, popping the top on his beer. He'd handed Lori his keys two beers ago. Lori wasn't drinking, as she was expecting their third child.

"And what circles do you frequent, Kyle?" Peyton asked.

"A colleague of mine has a son who, unfortunately, has gotten into a lot of trouble and has had several different parole officers."

"Max is the greatest guy," Lori added. "And his wife Fern, an unbelievable, kind woman. How their son ended being a serious drug dealer confounds us all."

"Anyway," Kyle said, "Max told me the parole officers his son Jonas had were nothing like yours. Sure, they didn't like him and knew he was a fuck-up and would continue to be, but they didn't harass him like Conway does with you. For the first few weeks they checked up on him all the time, once at night, but no later than ten thirty. And they certainly didn't trash his place like Conway does yours."

"What he does is just not right," Lori said. "He needs to be reported. I know you told us to stay out of it, and as your friends we are. But we also love you, and we worry about you and what he might actually do."

Warmth flowed through Peyton at the honest concern of her friends, especially Kyle. Lori, she could understand, since she'd known her over fifteen years. She'd only met Kyle right before Lori married him seven years ago, and that was through thick, bullet-proof glass at the prison.

Peyton walked over and gave both of them a kiss on the cheek. "I love you guys too, and what you helped me with tonight will make it possible to do what I need to when I'm released from him. Now, you two get out of here, turn your babysitter loose, and have wild monkey sex. You know you want to."

Lori laughed. "God damn, Peyton, you're so right. I think Kyle keeps me pregnant because my hormones are off the chart."

Kyle kissed his wife on the top of her head. "Dang, busted. But now that you mention it," he said, pulling his wife to her feet and tugging her toward the front door, "that sounds like a great idea."

Peyton was happy for her best friend. Would she ever feel the same? Would she ever want to?

Chapter Fifteen

It was eight o'clock, and Olivia's birthday party was in full swing when Peyton arrived. She still felt a bit uncomfortable with Olivia's family, but Olivia's mother Grace and her sister Fran went out of their way to make her feel welcome.

Olivia's father inquired about the club and her clients, and had asked Peyton several times for recommendations for improvements. He'd implemented several of them, and two more were on the drawing board to begin next fall. Peyton's suggestion to offer discounts to collegiate golfers increased their sales by eight percent and provided a stream of new business as they brought their friends and family to play at Copperwind.

"Peyton," Grace said, pinning her in the kitchen when no one was around. "I hope you know that we would welcome anyone you brought into our home."

To say Peyton was stunned was an understatement. The subject of her sexuality had never come up in conversation, but then again, she had no idea what Olivia and her mother talked about behind closed doors. As much as she'd come to love Olivia, a flare of anger surfaced that she and her mother had discussed her.

Grace placed five perfectly manicured fingers on her arm. Peyton instinctively stiffened at the unexpected contact, then relaxed.

"I know what you're thinking, Peyton. Olivia and Marcus haven't said a word about you that wasn't respectful or supportive. I may be old, but I'm not blind. I was waiting for the right time to tell you myself. It was too important to have Olivia be the go-between. Do you understand?"

The woman's sincerity touched Peyton, and she laid her own unmanicured, callused fingers on top of Grace's. "Yes, Grace, I do, and thank you."

"Peyton," her sister Natalie asked as she entered the kitchen. "Have you heard from Elizabeth?" Natalie and her husband had been invited to the party, as well as Peyton's parents.

"No, I haven't," Peyton replied, quickly stepping away from Grace, feeling awkward and self-conscious.

"I've left her four or five messages, and she hasn't returned any of them. I don't know if she's mad at me or what. But then again, she's always mad at me."

"She's always mad at everybody," Peyton commented.

"I know. I'm afraid for her, P," Natalie said, using the nickname she'd given Peyton when she was a baby.

"I'll go by and see her tomorrow," Peyton said.

"And you need to read her the riot act. She hasn't talked to Mom and Dad either, and they're smoking mad."

"You have such a way with words, Natalie," Peyton said teasingly.

"I know. That's why I have a 97 percent conviction rate," Natalie said, pretending to look down her nose at her and Grace.

"What about the other 3 percent?" Grace asked.

"Come on," Natalie said, ignoring the question. "Olivia's ready to cut the cake, and she won't start without you two."

"Elizabeth, open up!" Peyton shouted to be heard above the blasting music coming from behind the door. It was three in the afternoon. She pounded again, this time with her fist. "Elizabeth!"

Peyton tried the knob and found it unlocked. "Fuck."

Her sister lived in a run-down apartment complex in an equally tired, old neighborhood where the landscape of choice consisted of peeling paint, weeds, and dead grass.

She slowly opened the door, standing off to the side. The last thing she wanted was for some idiot to shoot her, thinking she was up to no good.

"Elizabeth, turn off the music." She eased her head around the doorway and didn't see anyone in the front room. She knew her sister had a roommate, sometimes more than one, and Peyton suspected the apartment was a flophouse. Gray duct tape held the glass together in several exterior windows. A baby cried, and the smell of burnt grease permeated the hall. The place reeked of neglect and despair.

She kept her hands at her side as she slowly went through the front room, kicking an empty pizza box that had long ago fallen off the table and onto the floor. She heard noises coming from the bedroom but checked the kitchen first, finding it empty. The sink was full of dishes, the garbage overflowing. A large roach scampered under a pile of dishes on the counter. Peyton shuddered and turned away in disgust.

By the sounds she heard as she went down the short hall, she knew what she'd find. She peeked around the door, and sure enough, there was her sister with some guy, a skull tattoo covering his entire back. Neither of them knew she was there until she pounded on the bedroom door. Both heads turned and looked her way.

"You're done," she said to both. She turned her attention to the guy. "Get your clothes on, and get your ass out of here." She pointed at her sister. "You get dressed, and get out in the front room."

"Who the fuck are you?" the man asked, climbing off the bed. Any intimidation he thought he had was diminished by the fact that he was butt-ass naked.

Peyton took three steps forward, effectively pinning him where he was. "An ex-con who just spent nine years in Nelson for murder, and I said get your ass out of here, NOW!"

The man's face went as white as his ass as he scampered around the room picking up his clothes. The last she saw of him was his bare butt as she slammed and locked the front door behind him.

While Elizabeth screamed obscenities at her from the other room, Peyton calmly pushed an empty beer box off a chair and sat down. A few minutes later, Elizabeth burst into the room tying her hair back.

"Who in the fuck do you think you are, coming in here like this?"

Peyton had turned off the blaring music, and it was finally quiet. "I'm your fucking sister. One of the members of your family that you have chosen not to return phone calls from." She looked around Elizabeth's apartment. Trash was everywhere, the carpet was stained, and remnants of four joints lay on the Coors beer can turned ashtray that was on the table. She didn't even want to know what was under the pile of stacked KFC buckets on the couch. "What in the fuck is going on here, Lizzy?"

"I told you not to call me that." Elizabeth snarled.

"I'll call you whatever I want. Right now, you're acting like a child."

"I'm nineteen years old."

"Big fucking deal. It's a number, nothing else." Peyton looked around the room, not even trying to hide her disgust. "What the fuck? This place is a pigsty."

"It's my place."

"You're right. It is your place, and it's not fine. If Mom and Dad were to come here they'd—"

"They've never come here—"

"Have you ever invited them? You know they'd never just drop by."

"You did."

"Yeah, well, somewhere in the last ten years, I lost my manners."

"What do you want, Peyton?" Elizabeth asked, her whine like a petulant child's.

"I want you to pull your head out of whoever's crotch it's in and get your life together."

"How dare you say that to me. You don't have any idea about my life."

"No, Elizabeth, I don't, and you have no idea how *I* spent nine years so you could sleep at night not having to worry if Chandler would come after you again."

"I didn't ask for your help then, and I'm not asking for it now," Elizabeth shot back, her face red with anger.

"Well, that's just too damn bad. We're family, Elizabeth, and family doesn't have to ask. We just do." And that was exactly what Peyton had done. Her sister had needed her, and she hadn't thought twice about it. "You've got to get some help."

"There is nothing wrong with me."

All that was missing from that statement was Elizabeth stomping her foot. "Look around, Elizabeth. Is this the way you want to live your life? Fucking one nameless guy after another."

"I haven't had any problems," Elizabeth said, lifting her chin defiantly. "Or complaints."

"Someday you will. I can guarantee it. Then where will you be?"

Peyton went home and spent the rest of her afternoon off looking through a photo album her parents had saved for her. All the pictures showed her and her family—a laughing, smiling group always having each other's back. She studied several of her and Elizabeth when she was just sweet, innocent Lizzy on her ninth birthday. Her smile was radiant, her eyes inquisitive and trusting as only a child's are. The next page and the page after that were empty, symbolizing how the lives of her entire family had changed that one fateful day.

Chapter Sixteen

You have a new client today, Peyton. You played in their foursome a while back, and she won a lesson in the silent auction at the foster-care benefit a few weeks ago."

"What's the name?" Peyton asked, holding her breath. Several lessons had been auctioned off that night, and she was afraid it would be Hilde. She'd spend more time deflecting her advances than teaching her anything.

"Leigh Marshall," Marcus said.

This time her heart did more than skitter. It actually jumped once or twice. "Okay."

"She'll be here at four thirty. She said she might be a few minutes late but will try her hardest to be here on time."

Having Leigh as a client entailed so many difficulties, the obvious one being Peyton's attraction to her. The not-so-obvious was that somehow Peyton had to get through the entire day before their appointment. She was scheduled on the beverage cart from seven to eleven, and then she'd do odd jobs around the clubhouse, intermixed with any other lessons she had to teach. Today she had three clients, two of which she spent only thirty minutes with, which would kill some of the time, but not nearly enough.

As expected, the day dragged on. Several people were peeved because she didn't have any beer; it didn't matter that it was only eight thirty in the morning. She raked out nine sand traps, emptied twelve cans of garbage, and gave her best effort, as she always did, for her clients.

The time between four and four fifteen crawled. She spent most of it looking at her watch and out the window to the parking lot. Finally, at four twenty-five, Leigh stepped out of the red Audi Peyton had seen enter the parking lot moments ago. "Nothing sexier than a good-looking woman in a hot car," she mumbled.

Leigh popped the trunk and replaced her golf clubs and duffel bag with her suit jacket and briefcase. As she hurried away, she waved her key fob in the air over her head. The taillights blinked and the trunk lid closed. She glanced at her watch as she hurried across the parking lot and through the front door, where Peyton lost sight of her.

By the way she was dressed, Peyton knew Leigh would be headed toward the locker room, where she'd drop her bag, change her clothes, and check in at the front desk. Peyton decided to wait for her there but didn't have to wait long.

Leigh hustled out of the locker room in a pair of teal-green golf shorts that ended just above her knees and a matching tank top with some sort of jungle pattern. Her golf shoes in her hand, her bag in the other, she headed toward Peyton in her sock feet. Peyton's pulse jumped as Leigh smiled when she saw her waiting. When she reached the desk, she dropped her bag and looked at her watch.

"Thank God. I wasn't sure I'd get here on time."

"You're fine," Peyton said. "I don't have anyone after you. Why don't you put your shoes on, and we'll head out to the driving range."

Leigh sat down on a bench across from Peyton. When she bent over to put her shoes on, her tank top gapped open in the front, giving Peyton, and anyone else who walked by, more than a little something to look at. Peyton knew her mouth was probably hanging open and she should do the respectable thing and look away, but it looked too good. Leigh stood up, but not before she caught Peyton staring down the front of her shirt.

Fuck. Peyton certainly hadn't wanted to get caught. She expected to see anger in Leigh's eyes, if not her refusal to have her as an instructor. Who wanted a golf teacher who, on their first meeting, leered at her student? Even though she was a little out of practice, what she saw instead was a flash of mutual interest before Leigh grabbed her hat from the top of her bag and pulled her ponytail through the back.

"All set?" Peyton asked, stepping forward, her voice a little huskier than normal. She picked up Leigh's bag.

"You don't have to do that," Leigh said, reaching for the strap.

"Part of the job. Come on. We'll talk as we walk."

Their golf cleats clattered over the tile floor and quieted when they hit the grass. The hard metal spikes on golf shoes had been replaced by star-shaped rubber cleats twisted into the bottom of shoes that looked more like tennis shoes or cross trainers than the ugly black-and-white ones during her playing days. Peyton grabbed two of the metal baskets of golf balls specifically used for practice. Each basket contained fifty balls with an orange stripe so as to clearly identify them as practice balls.

"I'm glad to see you're cashing in your winning," Peyton said, referring to Leigh's lesson certificate.

"I'm not one known to throw away money. That, and I could use a few lessons."

"Financially smart, that's good," Peyton commented. "So, what can I do to help you?"

"I'm not really sure. You saw me collapse when I played with Stark, and I'd like to understand how that happened. I'd certainly like to have my drives be longer and two putt instead of three or four."

Peyton was glad Leigh's golf bag was between them, giving her head some extra air to clear. When Leigh had passed her earlier, Peyton had caught a whiff of her perfume and become a little light-headed.

"Okay. Jill mentioned that you had some important round coming up."

Leigh's head snapped toward her, anger crossing her face.

"I'm sorry," Peyton said quickly. "Did I speak out of turn?"

"No, sorry, it's not you. For being my BFF, Jill has the biggest mouth on the planet."

"I wouldn't hold that against her. I got the impression she was just making conversation."

"Well, she needs to figure out something else to talk about besides me. But yes, and no. I have a round scheduled with my boss, but it keeps getting pushed back. Our executive team plays a lot of golf, and I need to step up my game. I don't want to make a complete fool of myself again."

Peyton chuckled. "I don't think there's any chance you'll make a fool of yourself, complete or otherwise. I've seen your game, Ms. Marshall, and it's pretty good."

"What's with the Ms. Marshall?" Leigh asked when they stopped at the practice position at the far end of the driving range.

"House rules. You're a client."

"What about Denise?" Leigh asked, referring to Peyton's client who had practically crawled all over her when they played a few weeks ago.

"She asked me to call her Denise."

"Well, Ms. Marshall is my mother, and you have my permission to call me Leigh."

"As I said, I've seen you play. You just need a little refinement, a tweak or two, and you'll be surprised how much your game will improve."

"From your lips to my body," Leigh said, imitating a golf swing.

Peyton dropped a basket, the balls scattering around their feet. Her pulse roared in her ears, her heart raced, her head started to spin, and if she were to squeeze her thighs together, she'd probably come.

"Oh my God, that's not what I meant. That didn't come out right. I'm sorry. I'm so embarrassed."

Peyton took advantage of Leigh putting both hands over her face to regain her composure. She concentrated on remaining upright and focused on her breathing.

"Don't worry about it." Peyton's voice sounded tight and controlled. "Let's start with your tee shot."

"Okay. Let me warm up. Next time I'll have this done before we start." Leigh pulled her longest club from her bag. She placed one hand on each end and slowly bent over at the waist, the club parallel to the ground. She let the weight of her upper body stretch her hamstrings until Peyton could see the curve of her back and imagine running her hands over the smooth skin. She raised the club over her head, extending her arms straight up and arching backward. Peyton's mouth was suddenly dry, the image of Leigh naked, straddling her flashed in her mind.

Peyton caught a glimpse of a colorful tattoo on the inside of Leigh's left bicep that she hadn't noticed earlier. From where she was standing, she couldn't see it clearly and certainly didn't want to get caught ogling her again. She filed it away for future reference if the opportunity came up.

Leigh repeated those moves four more times before using her club as a cane. She grabbed her right ankle and pulled her foot backward to touch her butt, stretching her quadriceps. She did the same for the other leg, then repeated the set four more times before holding the club behind her neck and twisting back and forth, each time turning farther than the time before. When finished, she stepped back and took several practice swings, slowly at first and finishing with a full-force swing she'd use to hit the ball. Peyton had counted the swings—anything to help herself keep her mind where it should be. Peyton was impressed by her warm-up routine and told her so. She was also more than a little aroused watching Leigh's body move. It was athletic and elegant, a very powerful, sexy combination.

"The last thing I need to do is hurt myself," Leigh said.

Peyton pulled it together. "Okay. Let's see you hit." Peyton handed Leigh a ball and one of the tees she fished out of her pocket. Leigh's ungloved fingertips grazed her palm, sending a jolt of electricity straight to her crotch. Peyton didn't dare look at Leigh for fear that what was going on between her legs would be evident on her face.

Leigh bent over, giving Peyton another tantalizing view down her top as she sank the bright-yellow tee into the grass. She set her stance, looked once down the range, and swung.

"Ugh. I hate it when I do that."

Her ball traveled only forty yards, its trajectory mirroring a rock skipping across the top of the calm pond.

"Try it again," Peyton said, not commenting on the obvious reasons the ball didn't catch flight and sail into the air.

Leigh's second and third shots were the same, and after she set her ball for the fourth, she turned to Peyton. She had one hand on her hip, the other on the end of her club. Her hip was cocked, her ponytail blowing in the light breeze. Peyton's breath caught somewhere in the middle of her chest.

"You make me nervous."

"Do you want a different instructor?"

"No," Leigh said after a moment. "You obviously know what you're doing, being the three-time NCAA player of the year."

A flush of adrenaline kicked in. If Leigh had Googled her, she knew her history—all her history. Leigh was here so it must not have scared her away. Or was it just curiosity like so many others?

"Every golfer looks at everyone else on the course," Peyton said, abruptly shifting her thoughts. "What brand of shoes you're wearing, how many clubs are in your bag, long putter or short. The worse their game, the more people look. You have to block it out and focus."

"Is that what you do?"

That's what I'm trying to do. "Yes. Just pretend I'm not here."

Leigh turned back and assumed her stance to hit the ball. "Like that's possible," she murmured loud enough that Peyton heard.

Peyton watched Leigh hit a few more balls. Her mechanics were fairly sound, but she needed to lower her ball on the tee, rotate her hips a bit more, drop her chin, and extend her follow-through.

"Hang on a second." Peyton knelt in front of Leigh. "Shift your hands a little," she said, putting her hands over Leigh's to move them to a more correct position. Heat burned through her, and she couldn't stop her eyes from raking a trail up Leigh's body and stopping at her eyes. Along the way she hesitated when she noticed that Leigh's chest was moving in and out faster than it had been before she touched her. Leigh's eyes flashed, and she loosened her grip on the club, almost dropping it.

Peyton regained control of her wayward thoughts and her runaway body and looked away from Leigh's mesmerizing eyes. "Just shift your right hand over a little more." Her voice was husky, and she cleared her throat. "Give it a try."

Would her body eventually get used to being near Leigh and stop reacting like this? Would she ever get used to her? Even outside in the middle of a driving range, tension filled the air. Peyton couldn't believe it was sexual attraction between them. It had to be due to her history.

Leigh's next few swings were awful. Obviously, Leigh was as shaken as she was.

"It might be uncomfortable at first, but you'll get used to it," she said, giving Leigh an out. Leigh mumbled something that sounded like "Yeah, right," but Peyton couldn't make it out. "Hit a few more. I want at least a couple dozen good shots before we move on. I'll look downrange if that makes you more comfortable. Just concentrate on where your hands are." *And I'll try not to think about where I want them to be.*

Peyton gave Leigh a couple of pointers on her stance and turning her hips but didn't touch her, even when, with other clients, she would have. The heat pulsing through her would probably scorch Leigh's clothes. Peyton stood on all three sides of Leigh observing her stance, her form, and her swing. She noticed a long, pale scar on the outside of Leigh's right knee she hadn't seen before. Even though she'd been distracted once or twice by Leigh's legs when they played, she had concentrated on her game so as not to embarrass herself in front of the women she was playing with.

Leigh's scar was faint, whereas Peyton's definitely was visible, a clear indication of prison versus private health care. It looked like her injury had been severe, and like her tattoo, Peyton couldn't comment on either. She was here to give her pointers on her form and her golf game, not what she saw on her body, however interesting it was.

Peyton made mental notes as she watched Leigh finish hitting the rest of the balls. Her club was perpendicular to her left arm, pointing slightly outside the ball—good. Her hands were almost in the right place on the club shaft—we'll work on that. Feet shoulder-width apart, weight evenly distributed between them—good. The ball was slightly out of line, but the clubface was looking at the target—something else to work on.

Her swing started in the right order. First the club head moved, then her hands, arms, shoulders, and lastly her hips. Her weight shifted correctly from left to right, but at the top of her swing, her club wasn't parallel to the ground. On her down swing, she lifted her head a little, her hips were too tight, and her left arm bent more than it should—all fixable.

"I think that's enough for today," Peyton said. She didn't wear a watch, but she had an uncanny sense of time and knew they had exactly five minutes left in their hour session. She wanted to give Leigh the opportunity to ask any final questions.

"How do you think you did? Did you see any improvement?"

"Yes, I did," Leigh said enthusiastically. "My hands were still uncomfortable, but the new grip made my drives straighter than they've been."

"Good."

"What do I do from here?"

"Obviously you can come back for another lesson or you can simply take what you've learned today and use it when you play. We can't cover everything in one session."

"I know. I didn't expect you to. I need to focus on one thing at a time so I can teach my body to remember what you told me to do. I'd like to see you a few more times. Maybe next week?"

Peyton's pulse raced at the thought. Obviously, the whole murder-prison thing wasn't a deterrent. "Okay. We'll go back inside and check our schedules and see what'll work for both of us." What she really wanted to do was learn every inch of Leigh's body.

Leigh returned her club to her bag, and peeled off the glove on her left hand, and put it back in the zipper compartment.

Peyton picked up Leigh's bag and slung it over her shoulder.

"How do you make it look that effortless?" Leigh asked.

"Practice. That and the fact that I do it all day, just about every day."

"How often do you play?" Leigh asked as they headed toward the clubhouse.

A shaft of pain shot through her at what she'd once had, then lost. "A couple times a week, I guess. Sometimes more, sometimes less. It just depends on what they need me to do."

"What a life," Leigh said. "Outside all day in the fresh air, getting a fabulous tan." Leigh's eyes lingered a few moments on Peyton's arms and legs. "You get to meet interesting people, no bureaucratic bullshit. Must be nice."

"It's a job, just like any other," Peyton replied. "Every job has its good days and its bad, but it's just a job."

This certainly wasn't what Peyton had envisioned during all those late-night hours studying her pre-med classes. By now she'd have completed medical school, her residency, and doing what she could to save lives. Instead, she'd killed someone, spent nine years in prison, and come out on the other side with her dream shattered, an unclear future, and dead broke. Not that she had any money when she was going to school, but her grandmother had left her some when she died, and Peyton had been counting on that to get her through medical school and to establish her practice. Instead, it went to her attorney. She wasn't angry or bitter. She'd made her decision and accepted the consequences, all of them, including where she was right now.

Peyton held the door for Leigh, and as she passed, Peyton caught another whiff of her perfume mixed with old-fashioned sweat. Some people might find it offensive, but not her. It was intoxicating. Peyton had always been athletic. She ran and lifted weights in Nelson not only to stay fit but to keep her sanity. Her schedule in Nelson gave her the opportunity to run several hours every day. By the time she was released she was barely winded after twenty miles. She'd even run a couple of marathons in the past few months. She hadn't won any of the races she entered, but she didn't need to. Running free in the warm sunshine was enough.

Peyton enjoyed running, now, especially since she had something to look at other than two twelve-foot-high, thick chain-link fences topped with razor wire separated from each other by thirty yards of soft sand. She was grateful that a fence surrounded Nelson and not the cement blocks found at other prisons. Outside the fence, for miles in every direction, was absolutely nothing. Every tree, shrub, and weed had been removed, and ironically, the low-escape-risk prisoners maintained the area in its pristine, sterile condition.

"Oh, man, that feels good," Leigh said when they stepped inside. It was hot today, and the air conditioner inside the club was a welcome relief to her as well. She was used to being outside all the time, and of course Nelson didn't have any air conditioners, so the heat didn't really bother her. Of course, if she had the choice of being inside or outside on a day with the temperature as high as it was today, she'd definitely choose inside.

"I'll get my calendar," Leigh said, heading in the direction of the locker room.

Peyton set Leigh's bag by the door and stepped behind a desk to the left, jiggling the mouse to wake up the computer. It had taken her a day or so to get the hang of the computer-based scheduling system, but now her fingers flew over the keyboard, pulling up her open times.

Leigh came out a minute later, her duffel bag over her shoulder and an iPad in her hand. She flipped open the cover and pushed the button. "Let's start with your availability," Leigh said, pursing her lips and frowning.

It took several times before they settled on the next five sessions, and after signing the voucher to put Peyton's fee on her bill, Leigh left the same way she came in.

Peyton watched Leigh walk to her car. Her head was high, her steps sure and confident. Leigh needed two attempts to get her bag into the trunk, and Peyton smiled at Leigh's earlier comment about the weight of her bag. Even though Leigh had a full set of clubs, it was lighter than most.

Peyton saw a car pull in and park next to Leigh. A man took his gear out of the trunk, but not before looking Leigh up and down completely. What was it with men that they couldn't just nod hello? Or simply not look? Yeah, right. Like she'd been able to keep her eyes off Leigh.

Chapter Seventeen

Leigh crossed the finish line, thrilled that she'd finished third in the race that qualified her for the finals to be held later this afternoon. Slowing down, she maneuvered her dirt bike through the other riders and stopped just outside the arena. She tugged off her gloves, putting them on the seat between her legs, unbuckled her helmet, and pulled it off. She slid the band out of her hair, running her fingers through it and shaking it loose.

Rick rode up beside her and slapped her on the back. If she hadn't been wearing her safety gear, it would have hurt like hell. However, the reinforced hard plastic surrounding her chest and back protected her from the force of his blow. Some riders didn't wear protective gear, whether from stupidity or thinking it didn't fit the macho persona of motocross riding. Leigh didn't care. Several times her protective gear, or as some called it, over-protective gear, had saved her from serious injury.

"Good job, Leigh," Rick said, his voice loud and gruff. "Steve's in the next race, and if he does well, we'll all be in the finals." Rick was referring to the remaining guy in their weekly riding group.

He rode off, and a woman seated in a red lawn chair next to a white cargo van caught Leigh's eye. The woman was about her age and had long, dark hair held away from her face by a bright-green visor. The day wasn't too cool for shorts, which showed off her long legs. The woman was looking at Leigh and smiled with obvious interest.

Leigh didn't wave but lifted her chin, acknowledging that she saw her. Even though she was sitting on top of the equivalent of two hundred and fifty horses, no way was she going to ride over to her on her bike, swing her leg over the saddle, and tip her helmet like in an old Western movie. She kicked the bike in gear and rode to where her truck was parked.

In addition to her Audi, she had a Toyota pickup that she used to haul her motocross bike and do other truck-like things that every lesbian needed. She stepped off the bike, lifted it, and set it on the stand. She set her helmet and gloves on the tailgate, reached inside the cooler in the bed of the truck, and pulled out a bottle of water. She took a few swigs, rinsing her mouth of the dust and dirt that somehow found its way there. She drank half the bottle before stopping to breathe, her thirst temporarily sated. She'd tried using a camelback, a water bladder secured in a backpack, but that was more problematic than it was worth. She was never able to get the tube that ran from the bladder into her mouth. The terrain on the courses was so difficult she needed to keep both hands on her bike. The first time she did it, she almost crashed, and the second, the tube ended up her nose. There was no third time.

She sat on the tailgate of her truck, raised her jersey, and pulled open the Velcro straps securing her chest protector, while her feet dangled in the air, inches from the ground. As soon as the fasteners opened, Leigh took her first deep breath since she put on the bulky safety equipment. She set it down beside her and tugged at the front and back of her T-shirt that had stuck to her like a second skin. Leigh finished the water before putting the heel of her boot beside her on the tailgate. She popped the buckles and slid her foot out of the heavy safety boot. She repeated the motion with her other foot and jumped to the ground. She slid off her heavy pants, stripping down to her tight spandex shorts. The cool air felt wonderful on her legs, and she placed the bulky pants beside her helmet. She opened the strap of the brace she wore on her right knee and slid that down her leg and off her foot. Leigh was rubbing her knee when she looked up and saw the woman approaching.

"That was a great ride out there," she said, stopping just in front of Leigh. The woman was slightly taller than Leigh, but her lean form made her look even taller.

"Thanks."

"I'm Tammy," the woman said, holding out her hand.

Leigh rubbed her hand on her shorts, looked at it, and said, "Leigh. Excuse the dirt."

As she shook the woman's hand, a predatory look flashed in her eyes. "I don't mind getting dirty."

Women had come on to Leigh before, but none nearly as blatant as Tammy. According to Jill and her other friends, sometimes she missed the signs completely. But there was no missing Tammy's intent.

"I'll have to remember that," Leigh said, her mind completely empty of any other reply.

"Obviously you've been riding for a while. You looked pretty good."

"Just something I picked up as a hobby."

"Quite a hobby."

Tammy was spending way too much time looking at Leigh's bare legs, and Leigh felt the heat of her gaze. She had a pair of cargo shorts on the front seat of her truck, but Tammy had stepped closer, making it next to impossible for Leigh to get to them. Tammy's eyes seared a path from the top of her knees to her collarbone, lingering on her chest, where her shirt clung to her breasts.

"You look pretty thirsty," Tammy said. "Maybe we could go somewhere and get something to drink."

"I have to race again later this afternoon."

Tammy eyes perked up. "Even better. Maybe we can grab a bite with our drink."

Leigh was tempted to say thanks but no thanks, but the devil on her left shoulder repeated Jill's words, "You need to get laid." An image of Peyton crossed her mind, and she quickly shut that thought down. That would not be a smart move.

"Sure, why not," Leigh said. "I should be done around five thirty."

"Five thirty it is. I'll come back here and find you." Tammy reached out and ran her finger from the top of Leigh's knee to the bottom of her shorts, burning a trail as she did.

Leigh wasn't certain Tammy was going to stop, and a thousand excuses ran through her head as she scrambled for the right one. She sighed in relief when the woman turned and walked back toward her chair. Tammy *was* very attractive. The devil on her shoulder whispered in her ear, "*You're gonna get laid,*" in a sing-song voice.

Leigh came in a respectable ninth in the final race. Twenty-four riders started, and after eight crashed on the third turn and six more at various places on the course, ten actually finished. She supposed it could be said that she came in next to last, but ninth sounded much better.

Tammy was waiting at Leigh's truck when she rode up. She was more attractive than she had been earlier this afternoon, and Leigh wondered how anyone could look that good after being outside all day.

"Have a good race?" Tammy asked as Leigh took off her protective gear.

"I didn't crash."

The woman laughed, her voice low and husky, sending chills down Leigh's spine.

"I suppose that's something. Wouldn't want you to get hurt."

Leigh's body heated, signaling that it needed some personalized attention as Tammy's eyes traveled over her limbs. "I'm in no condition to go out anywhere without cleaning up first."

"You can clean up at my place. I'm not far from here." Tammy's meaning was very clear.

"I appreciate that, but I don't have any clothes to change into."

"Who said anything about getting into clean clothes?"

"*You're gonna get laid,*" the devil said again. "How about I meet you somewhere? Maybe Michael's, on Twelfth and Broadway?" The restaurant was not too quiet to be intimate, but not too noisy so conversation was difficult. The woman appeared disappointed, and it looked like she might try to convince Leigh otherwise, but she said, "All right."

"Give me about an hour?"

"Of course, but I won't say take your time."

For the second time, she watched the woman walk away. *"You're gonna get laid."*

Leigh hurried home and parked her truck in the garage. She showered and grabbed the first thing in her closet, walking through the front door of the restaurant in fifty minutes. She stopped just inside to let her eyes get used to the darkness and sensed movement beside her.

"I hope you don't do everything this fast."

Leigh wondered if everything Tammy was going to say tonight would have a double meaning and decided to come right out with it.

"Your seduction has worked, Tammy. Any more and I might think you're desperate." Even though Leigh was a little out of practice, she cruised Tammy's body with her eyes. "But if you expect me to do anything other than fall asleep in my plate, I have got to eat."

Tammy smiled happily. "I love a woman who knows exactly what she wants and says it. Shall we?" She held out her hand, indicating for Leigh to lead the way to the hostess stand.

"You're gonna get laid." Leigh felt Tammy's eyes on her ass as they walked to the table.

Dinner was enjoyable or, more accurately, the food was good. Tammy turned into someone who could do nothing other than talk about herself. She was an investment banker, and Leigh wasn't sure if Tammy was salivating over her chest or how much money she made every month in commissions. She pitched a couple of deals Leigh's way, and it was all Leigh could do not to go to the ladies' room and not come back.

As Tammy droned on about something, images of Peyton flashed through Leigh's mind. By the end of dinner, Leigh found that she had pretty much compared the two women on just about every item. Tammy was tall, Peyton was taller. Tammy had long, dark hair, and Peyton's was short. Tammy eyes were brown, Peyton's an unusual aquamarine. Tammy's hands were smooth and manicured; Peyton's nails were short, unpolished, and had a few small scars.

Tammy's smile was forced, but Peyton's filled her face. Tammy was dull and lifeless when she talked, yet Peyton seethed with energy when she did. Tammy was nothing more than a pretty face and a hot body. She had nothing interesting to say. Leigh suspected there was more to Peyton than that, and she suddenly wanted to discover all of it.

CHAPTER EIGHTEEN

G od damn, that's good." Peyton set her coffee cup on the table in front of her. She'd run her usual five miles this morning and, after a quick shower, had made herself four slices of thick-cut maple bacon, two eggs over medium, two slices of wheat toast with strawberry jelly, and a full pot of coffee. She was always up early enough to sit and enjoy her home-cooked meal and not scarf it down in a noisy prison cafeteria. She had fixed herself the same breakfast every day since being released from Nelson, grateful to be away from something they called bacon but was almost unidentifiable, and if she ever saw another bowl of oatmeal, it would be three lifetimes too soon.

Good food at Nelson was virtually nonexistent, decent food, spotty at best, and a delicious cup of hot coffee was only a dream. The prison was required to serve nutritionally balanced meals, but their definition of nutrition was spelled fat, carbs, and processed. If inmates arrived at Nelson thin, they got thinner. If they walked in carrying a few extra pounds, they had several dozen more as they walked out. Food was a necessity to live and a hardship to eat. Peyton had quickly lost twenty-five pounds and had worked off an additional fifteen over the next few years. She'd kept it off by exercise and willpower, both, along with time, in abundance at Nelson.

She made a note to get her hair cut today. The Sport Clips she went to closed at nine, and she'd stop by there on her way home after work. Before Nelson, Peyton had worn her hair long and straight, like all her teammates. On match day, they would take turns French-braiding it, and they had matching blue and red bows in their hair. During Peyton's second week at Nelson, an inmate grabbed her hair and used it to drag her across the floor. She screamed, more from pain than from fear. She often wondered what would have happened if a guard hadn't stepped in and broken it up. The offender went to solitary and Peyton straight to Ruth Grayson's cell.

Ruth, a forty-two-year-old woman from Wisconsin, was a lifer. She'd killed her husband and his girlfriend when she came home from work early one day and found them in their bed. To make matters worse, the girlfriend was eight months pregnant, causing them to be very creative when it came to inserting Tab A into Slot B.

Ruth had established herself as the resident beautician. She didn't have a license or go to cosmetology school, but in prison, you couldn't be too choosy. A basic haircut cost five cigarettes, a cut and curl, ten, and anything with chemicals was a carton. Peyton walked in with hair down to the middle of her back and a full pack of cigarettes and walked out with eleven left and leaving all but an inch of her hair on the floor. Her mother gasped in shock when she saw Peyton the first time.

On her third week inside Nelson, four women cornered Peyton in the laundry area. She knew she was in trouble when one stood back as lookout and the other three advanced on her. They beat her severely, shouting taunts and threats interspersed with their fists and feet. Going in, Peyton knew she'd have a hard time. Her notoriety in the press did nothing to ingrain herself into the prison population. Even though some considered her a hero for killing someone at the bottom of that cesspool, it quickly became clear that her actions didn't guarantee her any special rights or privileges once inside. She hadn't been raped during that assault, but she'd lost seventy percent of her hearing in her left ear, and a deep cut on her cheek was stitched up in the prison infirmary, leaving a three-inch scar. She didn't get a hearing aid until she got out.

The Nelson Correctional Institution for Women had been built eighteen years earlier as the female inmate population soared, due to mandatory sentencing and more women making bad decisions and hooking up with worthless men. With over two thousand inmates, Nelson was one of the largest prisons in the country. Sitting on six hundred acres in the middle of nowhere, the massive facility had its own power-generation facility and a staff of eighteen hundred. Thirteen towers surrounded the facility, guards keeping a watchful eye on the grounds, ensuring the inmates stayed in and their accomplices out. Two guards armed with high-powered rifles and standing orders to shoot staffed each tower.

Nelson was composed of four wings, A-D, each with the capacity of five hundred prisoners. There was a cafeteria in each wing, as well as a laundry facility, small library, and rec room. On the grounds outside B wing were four basketball courts, two sets of free weights, three dozen cement picnic tables, and as half as many Ramadas. Every square foot was in the direct line of sight of at least two of the guard towers.

There was a revolving door of guards in the B wing at Nelson. The warden believed that rotating the staff kept them from becoming too complacent or getting too close to the inmates. Three supervisors assigned to B wing the entire time Peyton was a resident were the only constant.

McCormick was sixty-three years old, balding, with an extra-large belly and permanently wrinkled uniform. He was good-natured, had kind eyes, and treated everyone decently.

Twenty-eight-year-old Johnstone stood well over six feet, had thick, dark hair, and more muscles than brains. Peyton had heard that he was a high school football star who barely graduated. The acne scars on his face and neck were a sure sign his defined physique was more from steroids than hours in the gym. His mercurial temper confirmed it.

Joanne Davidson was a five foot-two-inch, hard-ass dyke who never gave anyone a break. She was often described as having the regulation book shoved so far up her ass, the words spilled out of her mouth when she spoke.

Peyton had had three cellmates during her stay as a guest at Nelson. Her first four years she bunked with Tina, convicted of armed robbery of a jewelry store a dozen years earlier. Tina was forty-three years old and had six kids, all with different daddies. Tina showed her the ropes and took care of her after she was beaten up.

After Tina was paroled, Rebecca moved in. Rebecca was serving a five-year sentence for selling oxy to other mothers in the PTA at her daughter's high school. She was a petite woman with long blond hair and a husband who visited her every week. Life at Nelson was completely out of her element. She was clueless as to what to do or how to survive. The first week, Peyton caught Rebecca wide awake, sitting on her bunk watching her.

On the third night Peyton told her, "Relax, Rebecca. I'm not going to rape you with a broomstick, or anything else, for that matter. I don't want a prison girlfriend, a best friend, or a paranoid cell mate. I'm only interested in doing my time with no problems and no drama."

Rebecca accompanied Peyton everywhere, as if she would protect her from the predators in their neighborhood. Peyton knew they were out there, just waiting for the opportunity to strike. She'd had to defend herself three times within her first forty-eight hours and twice since then. With someone as naive and privileged as Rebecca, it was only a matter of time, and she didn't want to be in the middle of that. On Rebecca's tenth day as her cell mate, Peyton told her that she needed to shower or she would find someone who would gladly "help" her. For the first year Rebecca cried constantly, and Peyton, metaphorically, entertained thoughts of smothering her with her pillow more than a few times.

Babs, her cellmate until Peyton was paroled, was sixty-eight-years old and had spent more than half her life behind bars. She had killed her neighbor with three shots to the crotch when his dog peed in her yard one too many times. She was tough, had a sailor's mouth and seventeen tattoos that Peyton could see, and didn't take shit from anyone. They got along just fine.

Shaking off unpleasant memories, Peyton headed for the shower. She'd replaced the hot water heater with the largest one she could find and often stood under the scalding spray until the water cooled. This morning was a quick in and out, and she started her day.

Chapter Nineteen

L eigh was fifteen minutes early to her second lesson with Peyton. When she signed in, Marcus told her that Peyton was just finishing up with her current client and would be in shortly. Leigh grabbed her bag and went outside, stopping just short of the empty putting green. She dropped her bag, pulled out her driver, and began her stretching routine.

She'd thought of Peyton every day since their first lesson, either when practicing her swing in her backyard or lying alone in bed at night. A few times her mind had drifted to her during a particularly boring meeting or conference call. Her body came to life every time as well, and more than once she took advantage of the privacy of her bedroom to release her frustration.

Leigh had had difficulty concentrating the last day or two, anticipating seeing Peyton today. She'd chastised herself more than once, but her body and mind refused to listen. This afternoon, she'd barely been able to sit still and forced herself not to leave right after lunch. She left at three, ran a few errands, and drove around the large block several times, sitting in her car for thirty minutes before finally allowing herself to get out and check in. She had no idea what was wrong with her. Her attraction to Peyton was borderline obsession.

"All warmed up?"

Surprised, Leigh spun around. Peyton had come up behind her, wearing knee-length shorts and a Copperwind polo shirt, topped with a Copperwind visor. She held a tall plastic glass of what looked like iced tea in her left hand.

The excitement that had tickled her stomach for days turned into drunken butterflies when she saw her. She couldn't remember having this type of visceral reaction to a woman in a very, very long time.

"Yep. All done. Traffic wasn't bad, and I got here early so as not to waste your time." Leigh knew she was rambling and forced her mouth to shut. Peyton smiled, and Leigh suspected she knew how nervous she was. God, get a grip, Leigh. You're thirty-seven, not a teenager.

"Great. Let's start on the driving range, and then we'll play a few holes." Peyton picked up her bag. "Did you play this weekend?"

Leigh had, and she gave Peyton the *Cliffs Notes* version but omitted how she had looked for her on every hole and how disappointed she was when she didn't see her all day.

"Okay," Peyton said, dropping the basket of balls onto the ground in front of her. "Let's see how you're doing."

Leigh set her tee and picked up a ball, all the while telling herself to relax. If she didn't, she'd make a complete ass of herself. That's all she needed to add to her ragged nerves.

Her first and second shots were pretty good, but her third veered to the right after Peyton reminded her to move her hands. They shook when she remembered Peyton touching her. Leigh wanted Peyton to tell her exactly where to put her hands—on her, not the club.

Peyton kicked another ball over to her, and Leigh didn't dare make eye contact before or after she placed it on her tee. She took a few deep breaths, adjusted her hands, and, without thinking any more about it, hit the ball.

"Good. Another." That was all Peyton said. After a dozen more balls, she picked up Leigh's bag and said, "Okay. Let's head out to the first hole."

On the way to the tee, Peyton asked Leigh to describe her game plan for the hole. Leigh checked the info about the hole on the placard next to the water cooler and rattled off the clubs she would use to reach the green. Peyton nodded her approval.

At the tee box, Leigh bent over to get a new tee and her ball from a bottom zipper of her bag at the same time Peyton stooped down to pick up a scorecard that had floated to the ground in front of Leigh's bag. Their heads were inches from each other, and they looked up simultaneously. Their eyes locked, and what she saw in Peyton's took Leigh's breath away.

Desire, passion, and raw need were clear, and there was no doubt Peyton wanted her. Given the way her body immediately responded, Leigh knew her eyes were conveying the same. Peyton's eyes moved to her lips, and Leigh knew she was going to kiss her. All she needed to do was lean in just a little, and their lips would touch.

Leigh was certain Peyton wouldn't make the first move, and she suddenly hesitated. Leigh always took charge of getting what she wanted in a sexual relationship. She wasn't demanding, but two people were always between the sheets, each with needs and desires that were expected to be fulfilled. Several seconds passed, and Peyton finally stood and stepped back.

Leigh grabbed her ball and tossed it onto the ground before Peyton could see how bad her hands were shaking. The connection she felt with Peyton was shocking. They'd spent only a few hours together. If she didn't pull herself together and focus, this was going to be a very long and potentially embarrassing lesson.

Fifty-five minutes later, Leigh felt she hadn't done too bad during the three holes she played. No way could she avoid Peyton or put distance between them. Peyton was always right beside her or behind her, making a comment or adjusting Leigh's body to the correct form. Peyton touched her hand, her hips, and even her knees while demonstrating a certain technique.

Peyton's fingers burned, and on more than one occasion, Leigh thought about doing something wrong just so Peyton would touch her again. She had difficulty concentrating on what Peyton was saying, let alone being able to actually do it. Leigh had caught Peyton looking at her more than once in a not-so-professional way, the tension from that first almost-kiss still between them.

They didn't say anything as they walked back to the clubhouse, and before she said or did something stupid, she made a beeline for the restaurant.

Peyton was behind the desk when Leigh exited and reached for her bag.

"I'll get it," Peyton said, picking it up and settling it on her shoulder.

Leigh wasn't sure if Peyton carrying her bag was chivalrous or ridiculous. Maybe a little of both. "Peyton, I can carry my own bag to my car."

"I know you can, but I'm headed that way. Besides, your hands are full." Peyton nodded at Leigh's hands that were, in fact, holding a large iced tea and a bright-orange bag of Crunchy Cheetos.

Leigh went out the front door, Peyton close behind, her clubs clinking together in the bag. In a few steps, she was beside her when Peyton asked, "Where are you parked?"

"Over there." Leigh pointed to a tan Toyota truck sitting in the last spot on the row. Actually, Leigh's truck was the only vehicle in the area where she pointed.

"Is this your bike?" Peyton asked, clearly surprised as they got closer.

One of the errands she'd run when she left early was to stop and pick up her bike from the mechanic. She knew she wouldn't have time to go home and drop it off, so she'd tossed her clubs into the passenger side of the cab before she went to work.

"Actually, I ride motocross." Leigh always got a cheap thrill when someone realized that. It wasn't that unusual for a woman to ride a motorcycle, but it was for it to be a Honda 250 dirt bike tearing around a dirt track with twenty guys.

"What's the difference?"

They had arrived at Leigh's truck, and she put the key into the lock and opened the passenger door. Her truck was over twenty years old and didn't have power locks. It didn't have power anything, other than steering.

"Motocross is riding a motorcycle off-road with hills and jumps and tight corners and short straightaways. The machine is a little different, more responsive and durable."

"Sounds pretty fast-paced and exciting."

"It is. It gets your heart racing and your adrenaline pumping."

Peyton thought of more pleasurable ways to get her adrenaline pumping. Especially with the woman standing beside her. "Where do you ride?" Peyton maneuvered her clubs inside Leigh's truck and closed the door.

"There's quite a few tracks around. It depends on where the guys want to go."

"The guys?" Peyton asked, her eyebrows raised.

"I ride with a club. There are six of us, and we take turns deciding where we'll go."

"Your bike looks pretty serious. How often do you go out?" Peyton looked over her bike. It was primarily red with a white rear fender and black seat. The tires were brand-new, the knobs still in place. The chrome shone from a recent wash.

"Two weekends a month."

"Wow. That's commitment," Peyton commented, still looking at her bike.

"Actually, it's a lot of fun, and because I spend so much time behind a desk, it's a great way to release that corporate tension. We're in racing season now, so most weekends we're on the track. This weekend we're at a race at Wild Horse Recreational Area over in Stanford."

"You race?"

Leigh laughed at Peyton's surprised expression. "Absolutely. You should come watch." Leigh stopped laughing, not sure where that invitation came from. It wasn't as though they were friends or that she was trying to be. She didn't know how the almost-kiss fit in. An awkward silence stretched between them.

"Thanks, I appreciate it, but maybe some other time," Peyton said quickly, stepping back from her truck like it was on fire. She turned away, but not before saying, "See you Wednesday."

Leigh tossed her duffel into the bed of the truck and watched Peyton walk toward the other cars in the parking lot. "You should come watch," Leigh said, mimicking her earlier invitation. "Jesus, Leigh. Could you have said anything more stupid?"

Peyton opened the door of an old Ford pickup truck and climbed in. It desperately needed a paint job, but from where Leigh stood, it looked like the body was in good condition. It started right up and didn't emit any black smoke from the tailpipe.

As Peyton pulled onto the main street, Leigh thought about her invitation for Peyton to come watch her race. Actually, it was more along the lines of you should come and watch the races, not you should come and watch *me* race. But still, why had she invited her in the first place? Was it out of habit and politeness, or was it something else?

CHAPTER TWENTY

"Turn your left hand a little," Peyton said, correcting Leigh's grip on her club.

"How? I'm over as far as I can and still hit the ball."

They'd been at the driving range for almost an hour, and Leigh was tired and hadn't been able to focus on anything Peyton told her. She hadn't slept much the past few nights. Dreams of Peyton straddling her on her motorcycle were keeping her from getting a good night's rest.

"Like this," Peyton said, stepping behind her. She wrapped her arms around Leigh and covered Leigh's hands with hers.

Peyton's body was directly behind Leigh, her hips snug against her backside, her breath warm against her neck. Leigh immediately reacted to the intimacy. She lost all track of what Peyton was talking about, felt only her hard body and soft breasts pressed against her. She relaxed into Peyton.

Leigh's heart was pounding, and surely Peyton could feel it. Peyton stiffened, then relaxed against her, then quickly stepped away.

"I think that's enough for today." Peyton's voice was husky, and Leigh thought she saw Peyton's hands shaking.

"Peyton," Leigh said, not really sure how to continue.

"Think about what we talked about today and what I showed you. Practice your grip and swing when you get home. Now, if you'll excuse me, I've got another appointment and have to get across town."

Peyton left so fast Leigh wasn't quite sure what happened. One minute she was helping her with her grip, and the next, all Leigh saw was her back as she practically ran toward the clubhouse.

Could she have been affected by their closeness as much as she was? Surely not? A woman who looked as good as Peyton had to have tons of experience with women. Leigh was sure she wasn't the first one to fall under her spell.

"What the fuck, Leigh?" she said, sitting down on the small wooden bench behind her. The sun was warm on her shoulders, and she reached for her water bottle tucked into a side compartment of her bag. Taking a long swig, she sat back, her mind running in different directions.

"Get a grip," she murmured quietly, even though there was little chance the overweight man in mismatched blue-striped shorts and green shirt hitting balls four spots over could hear her talk to herself.

"Okay. Let's sort this out," she said, her logical brain taking charge. "First, yes, I'm attracted to Peyton. Who wouldn't be? She's striking and I'd have to be dead not to notice. Nothing wrong with that, a perfectly normal reaction. Good God. It's not like I'm going to have a fling with my golf instructor. How clichéd would that be?"

Leigh paused to gather her thoughts. "Plus, we're in two very different places. I live in corporate America, and Peyton works at a golf course." Leigh cringed, because as soon as she said it, it sounded like they lived in a class-system society where she was the aristocracy and Peyton a mere commoner. Certainly she hadn't turned into a snob, had she? She hoped not.

"Okay. We're very different. There, that sounds better," she said to herself, nodding. "What do we have in common other than the love of golf?" Leigh listened to the whack and tink, the sounds of clubs striking balls, and they were somewhat soothing.

"I have no idea what we have in common. We don't talk about anything other than golf, but that's exactly what I'm paying her for—to help me better my game, not be someone to talk to socially. That's what Jill's for, and my sister Susan, and all my other friends."

Leigh stopped talking to herself, frustrated. She didn't remember how she even got on this conversational track. She needed either a long, cold shower or a long night with a beautiful woman. She gathered her gear and headed back toward the clubhouse.

❖

Peyton knew she'd just made a fool of herself, both in her reaction to Leigh's body against hers and then by making up some lame excuse to get out of there before she did something stupid like lick her neck, or worse. She'd learned how to mask her emotions; her mere survival sometimes depended on it. But her loss of control with Leigh had snuck up on her. One minute she was showing Leigh where her hands needed to be, and the next all she could think about was having her hands on her.

Peyton paced back and forth in the staff locker room, her nerves a mess. Another place and another time she'd have been all over Leigh. She'd have whispered something sexy in her ear and suggested they go out for a drink or some other prelude to sex. But this wasn't then. This was now, and she had much, much more to lose. She had to regain control. She was at the top of that very slippery slope, and she refused to let herself slide down, however much she wanted to. Want had nothing to do with it. It hadn't for nine years, and she wasn't about to let it cloud her mind now.

"Olivia asked me to invite you to dinner Friday," Marcus said thirty minutes later, when she finally emerged from the employee locker room. She was standing beside him checking her schedule for tomorrow.

"I know you're probably busy. After all, you are single, and even though I'm your brother and shouldn't even say this, you're dangerously attractive and most likely already have plans."

Peyton slowly turned and looked at him, raising her eyebrows. "Dangerously attractive?"

Marcus held his hands up in front of him defensively, his face flushed, embarrassed. "Not my words. Like I said, I'm your brother.

It's bad enough to even think my sister has sex, but I'm not stupid, even though Olivia says sometimes I am blind."

Peyton loved her brother for trying to lighten her mood. He had a way of knowing when something was bothering her, and something was definitely bothering her. Every time Marcus had come to visit her at Nelson, Peyton had returned to her cell in a much more relaxed state than when she left. She loved her brother and didn't know what she would have done if he didn't come to see her as often as he did.

"Stop rambling and get back to the dangerously attractive descriptor. I kind of like it." She enjoyed watching him squirm.

"It was a descriptor in one of Olivia's romance novels she reads."

"And how do you know this? Been peeking? Need some pointers for the boudoir?" Peyton was rewarded when Marcus obviously grew flustered at her implication. His eyes looked everywhere but hers, and he had that nervous fidget she remembered from when they were kids.

"What? No. No. I don't need any help in that area, thank you very much."

"I know. Olivia told me. I'm just rattling your chain." Peyton playfully punched him on the arm as if saying, You go, boy.

"She what?" Marcus asked, his eyes wide open.

"What do you think we talk about when you're not around? Recipes? You know I don't cook. But I do have sex, and so does she, quite often, if what she says is true." She punched him again. "We have to talk about something." She released her brother from his misery when she said, "Now back to this dangerously attractive descriptor. What exactly does that mean?"

"How would I know? Something about how girls could fall hard for you." He ran his fingers through his hair, a nervous gesture. "Since you and Olivia talk girl talk, you can ask her. Friday, *after* dinner, when you two go out on the patio and I'm in the kitchen cleaning up."

"She did say you have good hands and know exactly what to do with them and when," Peyton said, giving Marcus a hip bump and sidestepping around him, laughing. Her mood had shifted, and she was still chuckling when she stepped onto the putting green where her next client was waiting.

❖

"I embarrassed the hell out of Marcus the other day," Peyton said after she and Olivia sat down on the patio chairs two nights later.

"How so? Even if it is easy to do." Olivia kicked off her shoes and put her feet on the table.

"Somehow we got on the topic of sex."

"Sex? Marcus? My husband Marcus? Your brother Marcus?" she asked incredulously.

"One and the same."

"You've got to tell me your secret. I can't get him to even say the word." Olivia sipped her iced tea.

"Well, actually it was about my sex life."

Thankfully they were outside because Olivia spit a mouthful of her tea all over the patio. After she stopped coughing she said, "*This* I've got to hear."

Peyton replayed the conversation she and Marcus had had, adding a little color to describe her brother's reaction to her teasing. "I thought he was going to have a stroke."

"I'm surprised he didn't. He's a prude about that sort of thing. But I suppose I shouldn't complain. He could be a crude pig, like some other guys we're acquainted with."

"I know, but I couldn't help myself. He's so gullible."

Peyton and Olivia shared a laugh before she said, "I do think you're dangerously attractive."

"I *know* I'm dangerously attractive," Peyton said, and they both laughed even harder.

When they'd settled down and a cool breeze ruffled Olivia's hair, she asked, "How *are* you doing, Peyton? Seriously," she added before Peyton could make a flippant comment.

"I'm doing okay." She saw Olivia turn and look at her. She faced her and said, "Really, Olivia. I am."

Olivia studied her for a few long moments, and Peyton was glad the sun had gone down an hour ago. She was still rattled by her reaction to Leigh and wasn't sure it wouldn't still be visible on her face. She'd kept the conversation light during dinner and her mind off Leigh, but now that it had turned serious she wasn't so sure. Her façade was slipping.

"How is Lori? You two been out much?"

Olivia and Marcus had told her that they were grateful Lori was getting her out and introducing her to people. Women, more specifically. They had said they didn't know any lesbians and couldn't help her in that area.

"She's great. Her baby is due next month, and she says all she does is waddle to the bathroom and pee."

"That's what I hear. Marcus and I are trying to have one," she said after a few seconds.

"Really? That's awesome," Peyton said and meant it. "He'll be a great dad."

"He's had a good role model. I love your father."

"I do too. I don't know what I would have done without him."

"He worries about you, you know. We all do."

The familiar crush of responsibility settled over her. She hadn't felt it in a few weeks and had thought she was over it. Someday. Maybe.

"You all have to stop. I'm out of Nelson, safe, and I'm getting on with my life."

"It's just that we know how hard this has been for you." Olivia put her hand on Peyton's arm.

No, Peyton thought. You have absolutely no fucking idea. "Really," Peyton said, taking Olivia's hand in hers and swinging her legs off the chair to face her. "I'm doing okay. I have my moments, but what I have now is more than I dreamed I would have. I have a great job and a place to live, thanks to you and Marcus, a good friend who stuck around, and parents who smother me with love. What more could I ask for?"

"Someone to share your life with," Olivia said quietly. "And don't give me any shit about no one wanting to be with an ex-con." Peyton kept her mask fully in place. "That's not in the cards right now, Olivia. Maybe someday, but not today, and I'm okay with that. I have to get my life together, where I want it to be, before I can add somebody to it. It wouldn't be fair to me or to her." Peyton believed most of what she said. The part about adding somebody to it was a pipe dream.

"You know we're here for you," Olivia said, a mix of love and concern in her eyes.

"I know, and I love you for it." Peyton kissed Olivia on the cheek.

"Hey, that's my wife you're kissing," Marcus said in a gruff, joking voice as he stepped out onto the patio.

"I'm just getting her warmed up for you later," Peyton shot back, and both she and Olivia started laughing at Marcus's expression.

Later that night, Peyton replayed Olivia's conversation in her head. She was lying naked on top of the sheets, the ceiling fan turning above her bed.

What *was* she going to do? Would she live the rest of her life without someone to share it with? Someone to go to bed with every night and wake up to? Someone she could let down her guard and share her fears and joy with? Someone who loved her regardless of what she'd done? Was there even such a woman like that out there? If so, would she want to introduce Peyton to her friends, her family, her work associates? What would their neighbors think when they found out she'd killed a man? What would they do?

The sound of a motorcycle going down the street filtered through her open window, and a collage of images of Leigh came to mind. Sitting on her bike, sweat on her brow, dirt on her chin, her hair cascading down her back, conquering a tough hill, skidding around a tight corner, swinging a golf club, concentrating over her putter, smiling at her, looking at her, leaning back against her.

Leigh was a dichotomy, a mix of contradictions. She was highly intelligent and had risen to the top in a primarily man's field. She was feminine, yet tough and not afraid to sweat. She played a gentleman's game and tore up the dirt on a motorcycle, for God's sake. She got dirty yet came to her lessons wearing a suit that probably cost more than Peyton made in a month. She drove an Audi and had an old truck. She was serious one minute, then laughing hysterically the next.

Peyton had tried to figure her out. Hell, she'd spent countless hours just like she was now attempting to put her in a familiar, nice, neat little box. She'd finally concluded that there was no box for Leigh. She was unlike anyone Peyton had ever known, and it scared her how much more she wanted to know. Maybe after their lessons were over and she was no longer a client, they could see where it could go. Peyton rolled over and punched her pillow. Yeah, and pigs fly.

Chapter Twenty-one

A familiar sound coming from her left drew Leigh's attention. She lifted her bag over her shoulder and headed that way. She was tired from hitting four buckets of balls on the driving range but still too keyed up to go home. She'd looked for Peyton after almost every shot, making her practice completely ineffective.

The sound repeated itself as Leigh stepped into a billiard room. Three tables were spaced evenly around the room, Peyton holding a cue stick surveying the table in front of her. She didn't give any indication she saw Leigh come in. She was the only one in the room.

"Nine-ball, corner pocket."

Peyton looked up, surprise on her face, then smiled. "And how am I supposed to hit that?"

"Simple." Leigh set her bag down and stepped over to the rack that held four other cue sticks. Her heart was pounding, reacting to Peyton's genuine smile. She took one down and held it out in front of her. Seeing that it was fairly straight, Leigh stepped up to the table, lined up the shot, and the nine-ball rolled into the corner pocket.

"How did you do that?" Peyton asked.

"Practice," Leigh replied, chalking the tip of her stick. "And basic geometry."

"Show me," Peyton said, more a request than a demand.

"How much have you played?"

"I'm just a hacker, I guess. Played a little in college at bars, that sort of thing."

"How good do you want to be?"

"The best I can be."

Leigh wouldn't have expected any different.

"Okay. Let's start with the basics. Pool is a game of angles and setup." Leigh went on to explain the nuances of shooting billiards.

"It's a lot like playing golf. You need to do the same thing every shot you take. Show me how you get ready to hit the ball."

Peyton picked up her cue stick and stood next to the table.

"Good. Your feet are shoulder-width apart, but you need to turn your feet to a forty-five-degree angle to your right. Good," Leigh said after Peyton shifted her feet. "Show me how you hold the stick."

Peyton picked up her cue stick and held it in her hand. Leigh poked her in the side playfully. "Not just how you hold it, silly. How you hold it to hit the ball." Peyton leaned over the table as if lining up to make a shot. "Do you do it that way every time?

"I don't know. I guess." Peyton shrugged.

Leigh moved behind Peyton, mimicking her position, her body draping over her. Peyton stiffened. Her body was warm, and God, she smelled good. An image of them in a similar position in bed made her catch her breath. When Peyton relaxed against her, she lost any idea of what she was going to say.

The heat from Peyton burned a trail through Leigh's body and settled between her legs. Her mouth suddenly went dry, and she had a sudden urge to kiss her.

"Your stroke needs to be smooth and purposeful," Leigh said, her voice husky with desire. With her hand on Peyton's, she slowly moved the cue stick back and forth, not connecting with the ball. The innuendo was powerful, and Peyton shifted just a bit so their bodies fit together better.

"I, uh, haven't had any complaints."

Peyton's voice rumbled in her chest, the vibration shooting directly between Leigh's legs.

"You need to focus and eliminate all distractions."

"Trust me. I'm completely focused and rarely distracted." Peyton's voice was warm. "I always try to be really good at whatever I do."

Slowly Peyton turned, and Leigh wasn't sure they were talking about pool anymore. Peyton's eyes were on her lips, and Leigh leaned down to kiss her.

"Peyton? Did you get—"

Peyton stood up fast, almost knocking Leigh over.

"Oh, sorry. I didn't know you were in here, Ms. Marshall. How are you?" Marcus asked, looking back and forth between them as if trying to figure out what he'd walked in on.

"I'm fine, Marcus, thank you, and I've told you many times to please call me Leigh," she said, moving back a few more steps and rubbing her hands together.

"Leigh was just giving me a few pointers on playing pool," Peyton said, obviously feeling the need to explain.

Marcus smiled at Leigh. "Good. She needs it. She is terrible. I win two, three dollars from her every time we play. No, wait," Marcus said, frowning. "Don't help her. Then she'll win."

"On that note, I've got to go. See you next week," Leigh said, looking from Marcus to Peyton before turning and hurrying out of the room.

"Did I interrupt something?" Marcus asked carefully.

"No. Like I said, she was just showing me the right way to hold the cue stick. Seems as though I've been doing it wrong my entire life." Peyton waved her stick in front of her before replacing it in the rack on the wall. "Did you need something?" Peyton asked, hoping to shift the conversation to something far less provocative than being in the same room with Leigh. It was getting harder and harder to maintain professionalism when she was around.

Chapter Twenty-two

Peyton had never heard of Wild Horse Recreational Area, but it was easy to find on the Google Maps app on her phone. It was about forty-five minutes from her apartment, and she spent the entire time wondering what in the hell she was doing. When she'd looked up the arena, she saw the advertisement for the race Leigh had mentioned. She'd read it out loud in her quiet living room.

Calistic Invitational, sponsored by Budweiser. Three days of nonstop excitement as over a hundred motocross riders compete for the fifty-thousand-dollar prize package. A one-mile, single-track course with deep valleys, steep inclines, and hairpin turns is one of the region's most difficult courses. Last year only twelve of the top twenty-five riders in the finals completed the challenging course, with Mason Hartley winning it all on the final day of races. "It was a great race," Hartley said after accepting the winner's trophy and a check for twenty-five thousand dollars. "The competition was great and the course challenging."

Peyton looked at the accompanying photos. Three guys were straddling their bikes in front of a large Budweiser sign, each holding a can of the sponsor's beer. Peyton made a face. She hated Budweiser, but if it was the sponsor of something she'd won, she'd gladly hold one. In each of her LPGA tournaments she'd learned that sponsors were where the big money was.

Peyton glanced though other photos on the site, looking for any sign of Leigh. The pictures, from last year's event, showed no sign of her. She scanned the list of participants and finishers, and her name didn't show up there either.

Peyton passed several temporary road signs informing her that she was getting close. Traffic slowed, then crawled as men in jeans, white long-sleeve shirts, and straw hats exchanged money for a parking ticket. One by one the vehicles in front of her inched closer to the attendants, and by the time it was her turn to pay, butterflies in her stomach accompanied her as she parked.

After paying a reasonable entry fee, Peyton walked around the event grounds. The facility was relatively new, having been built while she was at Nelson. It wasn't fancy—a few solidly built buildings, rodeo grounds, several horse trails, a long row of unisex toilets, and several sets of viewing stands.

Trucks, some big, some small, were parked haphazardly in a staging area to her left. Motocross bikes in all colors and sizes leaned against them or sat atop stands that looked like modified jack stands. Peyton quickly saw that the bikes didn't have the typical kickstand to hold them up. What a pain in the ass that must be, she thought.

Paying an outrageous amount for a can of Coke, Peyton avoided the staging area and strolled around the grounds. She wasn't hiding but didn't particularly want Leigh to see her either. A couple dozen vendors under white shade tents were selling everything from home-grown peanuts to riding gear and stickers proclaiming the name of the event. She stopped at one of them, and a man started talking.

"This is the newest jersey from Fox Racing. It's made of moisture-wicking fabric with vented side panels for enhanced airflow. The pants…" The man pulled out a hanger from a round carousel. "The pants are rider- and attack-position constructed. They have heat and abrasion-resistant leather knee panels and stretch panels at the knee, rear, and crotch. These here," he pulled out a different hanger, "are designed to fit the female body."

Peyton had some idea of what he was talking about, but when he continued his sales pitch about the socks, she had to ask.

"Motocross-specific socks?" she asked skeptically.

"Absolutely," the man said, not the least bit ruffled. "They won't slip down into your boots and give you blisters. And like the jersey, they're made to wick the moisture away from your feet." He laid the pants on top of the rack and hurried to another one. "We have both the under-jersey and over-jersey body armor. We're the only vendor here today that carries one specifically for women," he said proudly.

He held up what looked like a brace one of her fellow inmates had worn after she broke two vertebrae in her back when she fell down the steps during a fight. Body armor? That was an appropriate name. This one was molded plastic in a deep shade of purple, with three Velcro straps in the front to tighten it and a curve in the plastic at the bust line.

"Just looking, thanks," Peyton said, stepping away and staying far enough away from the other booths not to get sucked in. The guy was nice enough but seemed a little desperate.

The crowd was picking up, and a large man in an even larger cowboy hat jostled her. "Sorry," she said, even though he should have been the one to say it; she was the one standing still. The man stopped and turned around, his beer sloshing over the rim of his white plastic cup. The wristband identifying him as already carded for alcohol barely fit around his beefy wrist.

"What did you say?" he asked, anger obviously just below his last beer.

"I said sorry," Peyton said, hoping this would go no further. The last thing she needed was a hassle at a motocross race.

"Damn right you are, bitch," he said slurring his words and continuing on his way.

"That looked like trouble," a voice behind her said.

Peyton turned, and a very attractive woman in tight jeans and a low-cut, red, silky blouse was watching the man walk away.

"Could have been, and I'm not looking for it," Peyton replied.

The woman shifted her eyes from the man to Peyton, starting with her eyes, down to her worn boots, then back to her eyes again.

"What *are* you looking for?" she asked, clearly a come-on.

"A cool place to sit and watch the races," Peyton replied. Judging by the obvious interest in the woman's eyes, a few weeks ago Peyton's answer would have been different.

"Here to watch anyone special?"

Peyton debated how to answer. If she said yes, the woman would probably back off. If she said no, odds were good she could have an enjoyable afternoon. It had been several months since she'd had "an enjoyable afternoon," or evening for that matter. She settled on something that might be the truth if she didn't think about it too long. "Maybe."

The woman looked at her for another long moment, as if sizing her up. Peyton had been sized up before by predators, women desperate for protection and those that were just plain mean. She didn't flinch.

"Well," the woman said, boldly running her finger down the center of Peyton's chest. "If 'maybe' turns into 'no,' my name's Cassandra, and I'll be around all day."

Leigh's shock at seeing Peyton in the vendor area was quickly overruled by a blaze of jealousy. Even from this distance, Leigh could see the woman talking to Peyton was interested in her. Who wouldn't be? With Peyton's long legs, trim build, and general walking sexuality, any self-respecting lesbian with eyes and a clit would want a chance at her. And, by the churning of the green monster in her gut, Leigh was obviously front and center in that category.

"Leigh, let's walk the track," Rick said coming up behind her. Walking the track was what riders did to familiarize themselves with the course. They looked at the starting line, how tight the turns were, and any blind spots or obstacles that could cause them trouble.

"We did that already." Then she thought better of her rude protest. "Sorry, Rick. Let's do it. The track has most likely gotten sloppy from all the riders this morning. It's probably pretty torn up by now."

They walked to the top of a hill adjacent to the course. The next heat was underway, and they watched the twenty riders maneuver their way up, down, and around the track. At least Rick watched. Leigh looked for Peyton.

Thirty minutes later, Leigh rode to the start line and took her assigned place in the middle of the twenty riders. She turned off her engine and looked down the first hill. The course at Wild Horse consisted of one mile of tight twists and turns, fourteen hills, three dry creek beds, and a lot of soft sand. The riders started from the top of a large hill, and the first turn was a sharp dogleg to the right at the bottom. Six or seven riders in the previous heat had dumped it on the first turn and never recovered to finish the race in one of the three spots to qualify for the finals.

To her left and right, riders got into place, each completing their own pre-race checklist. She adjusted her fuel knob and the buckle on her helmet. She stomped her boots on the ground, adjusted her gloves, and reset her goggles. When the guy in the blue shirt told them to start their engines, she was ready. She was mentally focused, having ridden the race in her head several times while sitting here. She kicked her bike into gear, ready for the gate to drop.

The gate looked like a bike rack, their front tires in between the metal bars. Instead of somewhere to chain up their bikes to prevent theft, the rack prevented any rider from jumping the start and getting an unfair advantage over the others.

A man in a pair of coveralls and no shirt waved a yellow flag. It was too loud to hear what he was saying. Leigh's stomach fluttered with anticipation. He dropped the yellow and raised a green one. Leigh's pulse raced a little faster. Several riders were pressing their front tires against the rack, throttles wide open. When the rack dropped, Leigh released the clutch.

Peyton had her hands over her ears as the first racers flew by. The noise was overwhelmingly loud, and she wished she'd thought of bringing ear plugs. She'd never been to a race or even watched one on TV, for that matter, and she had no idea what was going to happen. She'd found an empty seat on the eighth row of rickety bleachers, the metal seat hot from the afternoon sun. A skinny man with a John Deere hat and a clear plastic cup of beer in each hand was to her left, a man in camo shorts and flip-flops to her right. Several heats had finished, and she hadn't seen anyone that looked like Leigh. But then again, in the helmets and bulky gear, everyone looked alike.

A flash of red shot by, and Peyton didn't know if it was Leigh or not. Several of the bikes were red like hers, but only one rider had a blond ponytail blowing out of the back of a purple-and-white helmet. Number thirteen, in the purple-and-white helmet and riding gear, had to be her. Peyton's excitement grew along with the crowd's.

At the first turn, Peyton gasped as several riders crashed, and she was able to breathe again when she saw how Leigh somehow manage to stay on the left of the rapidly forming pile of spinning wheels, arms, and legs. As Leigh approached the first hill, she had her knees flexed to absorb the shock from the bumps in the track. As she flew over the top, her legs acted like springs to cushion the landing. Peyton felt her body rise and fall, mimicking Leigh's actions.

As Leigh approached the next turn, Peyton held her breath when she stuck her leg out as if she might need it to balance or touch the ground if she was about to fall. Great way to break a leg, Peyton thought. Leigh picked up speed and repeated the same maneuver over several other hills. On the last one, her tires left the ground, and she literally flew through the air, landing with a jolt Peyton could feel in her bones.

Dirt kicked up behind her as Leigh rounded the next curve, her back tire fishtailing before she got it back under control. She rode through a puddle of mud before executing another hairpin left and right turn before racing down the back stretch. More riders were in front of her than behind, but Leigh kept up and passed one on a series of left and right turns. She crossed the start/finish line, heading for the treacherous first turn. At least Peyton thought it looked good. Lap after lap Leigh kept after it, slowly passing each rider until more were behind her than in front.

As a former athlete herself, Peyton knew Leigh had to be in top shape to take that kind of physical pounding. The mental challenge and concentration of constantly having to adjust to the change in the track and knowing where the riders were around you had to be exhausting.

Peyton cheered as Leigh passed another rider, and the man beside her offered her a pair of earplugs in a sealed bag he'd fished out of his front pocket. She nodded her thanks, the noise far too loud for any conversation.

Twenty minutes later, the same guy in the overalls waved a white flag as the riders flew by. One more lap to go and Leigh was in sixth place overall. When Leigh crossed the finish line, in seventh place, Peyton cheered along with the rest of the crowd.

The spectators in the stands started shuffling down the metal steps, the excitement for the day over. Peyton guessed there would be some type of ceremony for the winners, and she joined the crowd as they moved en masse toward the front gate.

A flash of purple caught Peyton's eye, and she turned to see Leigh slowly riding past on her way to the staging area. Before she could think about it too much, she followed her. "Excuse me. Excuse me," Peyton said several times, trying to get out of the flow of the crowd. When she was finally on the perimeter she could move more quickly, and she veered to her left.

Peyton remembered that Leigh drove a small tan truck, but it was hard to find in the sea of macho lifted trucks, motorcycle trailers, and pop-up shade canopies. At least they had parked in semi-straight rows, and she had to walk down only three before she saw her. Peyton hurried her pace.

Leigh was silhouetted in front of the sun, and Peyton froze when Leigh pulled off her helmet and ran her hands through her hair several times. She was beautiful in her riding gear, clunky boots, and body armor. Peyton had always had a thing for athletic women, and if she thought Leigh was attractive on the golf course, she was smoking hot on her bike.

Leigh glanced around, and Peyton's pulse skidded to a stop when their eyes met. All the chatter, horns, and revving motorcycle engines drifted away, and she heard nothing but the pounding of her heart. Her mouth was dry, her entire focus on Leigh. Peyton couldn't remember the last time someone had her complete, undivided attention, if ever. Before Nelson she had always been multitasking in everything she did. She was always with her friends or teammates, studying for exams or practicing. She'd had girlfriends on and off during college, but she'd felt nothing like what was coursing through her now. Leigh's face lit up when she saw her, and Peyton could barely breathe.

"What are you doing here?" Leigh asked, hanging her helmet over the right side of her handlebar. She stuffed her gloves inside her helmet.

"Peyton?" Leigh asked again, this time concern on her face.

"Oh, yeah, right." Peyton closed the distance between them. "How did you learn to do that? To ride like that?" she added, if there was any doubt what she was referring to. Obviously, Peyton knew Leigh rode, but nothing had prepared her for what she'd just seen on the dirt track.

"Practice," Leigh said. "Lots of practice. I even have the scars to prove it."

"Is that what happened to your leg?" Damn, Peyton thought. She shouldn't have brought that up.

"Yeah. Three years ago. I was taking a corner, and my leg decided to go the other way."

"Looks like it hurt," Peyton commented.

"Only when I breathed," Leigh said blandly.

"How long have you been riding?"

"I started in high school. My dad said I had my nose in a book too much and needed an outlet to refocus on."

"I'm impressed."

"Why? It's just riding a motorcycle around a track."

Peyton was puzzled at Leigh's sudden change in demeanor. She'd been happy to see her, and now she was sarcastic and curt. "And the US Open is just a round of golf on a municipal course."

"Touché."

Leigh lifted her jersey and opened the Velcro straps on her body armor. "I don't want to keep you."

That was a brush-off if Peyton had ever heard one, but she wasn't put off that easily anymore.

"Did I do something wrong by being here?" Peyton asked, her anger starting to pulse. "Because you asked me to come, unless you were just being polite and feeding me bullshit."

Peyton cringed inside, but it was too late to take her remark back. That would probably cost her Leigh as a client and maybe her job. No. That was too harsh. Her job wasn't involved with this conversation. This was personal.

"No. Not at all."

"Then why are you trying to get rid of me?"

"I'm not trying to get rid of you."

"Bullshit."

"Excuse me?" Leigh asked, a surprised look on her face.

"You heard me. I call bullshit."

Leigh tugged off her body armor and pulled her jersey back down, hiding the perfect curves of her breasts.

"Look, I'm sorry if I was short with you. I'm tired, and I'm sure someone's waiting for you so, thanks for coming, and I'll see you next week." Leigh swung her leg over her bike and leaned it against her truck.

"What? Who? I came by myself. I don't have anybody waiting for me." Peyton was totally confused.

"I saw you talking to a tall, gorgeous woman with red hair. She seemed pretty interested in you."

"Who?" Suddenly Peyton realized who Leigh was talking about. The woman who came on to her before the race. The thought that Leigh saw that and was pissed was interesting. "She came on to me," Peyton said, and it sounded too much like she was defending herself. "I don't even remember her name."

"Well, she sure wanted your number." Leigh bent over to unbuckle her boot.

"I didn't give it to her. I didn't even tell her *my* name. She's not my type."

"What is your type?"

You. "I'm not in the market for a relationship."

"I don't think a relationship was what she was looking for," Leigh said, sliding off her boot.

"Are those the special motocross riding socks?" Peyton asked, just to throw the conversation in a different direction.

"What?" Leigh asked, obviously confused.

"Your socks. The guy in one of the booths was trying to sell me some socks made specifically for the sport. I wasn't sure if he was jerking my chain or not."

"No. These aren't special motocross socks. They're just plain old Nikes. However, Rick, one of the guys I ride with, swears by them."

Peyton didn't say anything else until Leigh finished putting on her cross-trainer shoes. She tied the laces and finally looked up.

"Leigh, I came to see you, not get picked up. When you said you raced I was surprised, and it piqued my interest. I thought I'd come take a look. Nothing more."

Leigh had the good grace to blush, a look Peyton found endearing.

"I'm sorry I overreacted. I had no right. I guess seeing you just caught me off guard. Thank you for coming."

"You're welcome," she replied, some of the tension easing. "It was really something. Do many women ride?"

"A few. Some of the wives do, but there's no reason we shouldn't have more."

"It looks like fun."

Leigh tilted her head, shading her eyes from the sun. "I can teach you," she said, their truce still a little tentative. "I can teach you," she repeated, this time with more enthusiasm. "It's easy."

"With you teaching, I'm sure it would be, but I really don't have any time." It was Peyton's standard noncommittal excuse.

"You had time to come here today."

"I work every weekend."

"Take a day off."

"We'll see," Peyton said vaguely.

"If I have time to take golf lessons from you, you have a few hours on a Saturday or Sunday to come ride with me."

Leigh stood with her hands on her hips, looking at Peyton like she wouldn't take no for an answer. Her confidence and attitude were more than a little sexy. And that worried Peyton.

CHAPTER TWENTY-THREE

L eigh's focus was in the toilet. Since the race last weekend, she couldn't get Peyton out of her head. Today was their third lesson, and they planned to play several holes. Peyton had said she wanted to see her game and how she hit the ball in various situations. It was late afternoon, and Leigh had teed off on the tenth hole thirty minutes ago, the golf course practically empty.

"Remember to watch the ball go into the hole," Peyton said as Leigh lined up her putt on the thirteenth hole.

Leigh stepped away from the ball and took a few practice swings, trying to get her body to pay attention to what Peyton was saying, not how she looked, how close she was, how good she smelled, or how many times she'd touched her since they started.

The first time was when she lined up on the tee, Peyton stepping in front of her to move her hands into the correct position. Their faces were inches apart, and Leigh swore Peyton's hands were on hers far longer than necessary. The second time was when Peyton put her hands on Leigh's hips to show her how they should shift when she hit the ball. Peyton was behind her, her warm breath on her neck. Leigh had no idea what Peyton had said and faked her way through the shot. When they reached the green, Peyton had moved behind her and wrapped her arms around her again, this time showing her how to smoothly stroke the ball into the hole. Their bodies were touching, Peyton's strong arms engulfing her. Leigh nearly dropped her club.

She froze, afraid that if she moved, Peyton would step away and even more afraid that she wouldn't. She wanted to lean back into her, feel Peyton's lips trailing kisses up and down her neck, her breath in her hair. Peyton's breathing became shallow and fast against her back, and Leigh knew she wasn't the only one their closeness affected. Desire flared, streaking out to her arms and legs. Leigh's fingertips tingled with the need to touch her.

Slowly she turned, still in the circle of Peyton's embrace. The air suddenly became very, very still. Leigh's body came alive. Every nerve tingled, and her senses shifted into full alertness. Her hands trembled when she cupped Peyton's face. Her skin was soft, her jaw strong, her eyes burning with desire.

Leigh was already aware that Peyton wouldn't make the first move. She was her client, and she would never cross that line. If anything was going to happen, Leigh needed to be the one to start it. She might even have to keep it moving if Peyton balked. By the look in Peyton's eyes, and her shallow breathing, Leigh doubted Peyton would need much convincing. She slid her hand behind Peyton's head, pulled her close, and kissed her.

Peyton's lips were soft and warm, almost tentative, but Leigh sensed driving passion barely restrained. Peyton's desire for her thrilled Leigh, and when she deepened the kiss, Peyton's lips became demanding.

Leigh moaned when Peyton's hands started to roam. When they slipped under her T-shirt, she was sure her knees would buckle. Arching into the caress, she instinctively grabbed Peyton's head, twisting her fingers in the short, dark hair.

Peyton's fingers ran up and down her side, passing lightly over her stomach and between her breasts. They were full, and her nipples ached to be touched. Leigh gasped in pleasure when Peyton's thumb brushed over one of them.

Peyton lifted her head, her breathing ragged. She grabbed Leigh's hand and pulled her to a stand of thick trees not far from the green. She turned Leigh around, pinning her back against the rough surface. Leigh didn't care. It had been so long since she felt the overwhelming need for a woman like this.

Peyton slid her leg between hers, and Leigh felt the wetness of her own desire. Peyton's actions were bold, and Leigh almost exploded when Peyton's hands found their way under her bra and pinched her erect nipples. One of Peyton's hands drifted down her stomach and slid under the waistband and into her in one fluid motion. The familiar burn started low in her belly and exploded before Leigh knew what was happening. Never before had she done something like this, certainly not this fast, and absolutely never where anyone could see her. All she could do was hold on as her orgasm rocked through her.

Leigh had no idea how long it was before her head cleared enough to realize what had just happened and her body to tell her it didn't care. She was still clinging to Peyton, her arms wrapped around her neck, her breathing ragged.

Peyton, trying to catch her breath, said, "We can't do this."

"A little late for that, don't you think?"

Peyton's fingers were still in her, and Leigh was far from finished. She was rarely a one-and-done girl, and if she wasn't careful she'd come again. Just thinking about Peyton's fingers made her clit twitch.

"We can't." Peyton repeated the words as if trying to convince herself.

"Then you'd better get your hand out of my pants."

Peyton stiffened as if she'd forgotten exactly where her hand was.

Leigh wanted to know what Peyton was thinking at this moment. Was she as affected by their spontaneous coupling as she was? Was her head spinning? Did she crave more? Was she excited, shocked, or scared shitless at how quickly things had escalated? Stunned that they had had sex on a public golf course? Was she reveling in the fact that she was a woman and all the pleasure that came with it? How thrilling it had been that desire overcame reason and she had no control to stop it? Was every nerve alive like never before, ready and needing to be touched again? Was she trying to make sense of what had just happened? To place it in a neat, comfortable place? To rationalize her completely irrational behavior? Did she want to chalk it up to hormones, pheromones, or some other chemical cause? Was she struggling with an event so impersonal yet so intimate? A connection so foreign she was grappling with how to describe it? Did she want to spend hours together discovering each other's body, their pleasure points, whether a firm hand or a soft caress would elicit a moan of desire or a whisper of need? Did she want to do it again? Forget it ever happened? Did the excitement of pure, raw sex thrill her to the point she lost her mind? Did she want to cast aside everything she knew, everything she thought she wanted to have, burning need fueled with just a glance, a touch, a memory? Did she want her old world back, her neat little everything in its place world, or did she want to jump into the abyss of the pleasure of a few moments ago? Were her knees weak and her brain stopped? Did she want one more kiss, one more touch?

"This can't happen again."

Leigh managed to disentangle herself from Peyton with some dignity. Why did she feel crushed? She'd been turned down before, hadn't been called back or asked to dance again. This wasn't like they'd been in a relationship she'd thought was going somewhere only to have the rug pulled out from under her. She'd had one-night stands before that had left her fulfilled, energized, relaxed. Then what the hell was her reaction to Peyton's words?

CHAPTER TWENTY-FOUR

S on of a bitch."
Leigh almost ran into Peyton as she dashed through the front door of the club. She'd just come out of the locker room, trying to pull herself together. Peyton was drenched, her clothes clinging to her body, leaving little to the imagination. A few minutes ago, Leigh had heard a thunderous clap, followed by the sound of torrential rain. It was still coming down. The clouds overhead during their lesson had been ominous, and it was obvious they'd made it back inside just in time, even after their little detour on the thirteenth green.

"Peyton, what happened? Are you okay?"

"My truck won't start," she said, wiping the rain from her face.

"Here," Leigh said, handing her a Copperwind monogrammed towel from a neat stack behind the scheduling desk.

"Thanks." Peyton rubbed the towel over her face and arms before mopping her wet hair.

Leigh couldn't help but notice how Peyton's wet clothes accentuated every curve. Her nipples were poking out from her polo shirt, and Leigh's pulse started to race. Peyton, fully clothed but soaking wet, was almost as sexy as she would have been standing there stark naked. Leigh remembered how good it felt to kiss her, be in her arms, feel her hands on her—hot, demanding fingers in her. She'd done nothing but think about it since it happened, a little less than thirty minutes ago.

"I'll take you home so you can change."

"What?" Peyton asked.

"You don't live far from here. I'll take you home and you can change into something dry, and I'll bring you back." During one of their sessions, Peyton had mentioned that she lived only a few blocks from the club. "You're shivering," Leigh said needlessly.

"You don't need to do that. I can get Marcus to drive me home."

"I saw him leave a few minutes ago. You probably just missed each other. It's no trouble, really."

As Peyton mulled over her offer, Leigh told herself to keep her eyes focused on Peyton's face and not her chest. Her brain refused to listen. Leigh hadn't been with anyone for several months, and their explosive encounter had reminded her how much she was missing. Peyton was a hot, desirable woman, no doubt about it. The tension between them hadn't diminished after their earlier encounter. To the contrary, she wanted more.

"Leigh?"

Leigh felt herself blush at getting caught staring. She grabbed one of the complimentary umbrellas in a stand beside the front door. "Let's go before it gets any worse."

It was still raining heavily as they walked across the parking lot, their shoulders and arms brushing as they navigated growing puddles. Leigh opened the passenger door of her car and held the umbrella while Peyton climbed in, then hurried around to the driver's side. She opened the door, retracted the umbrella, and hopped in all in one motion.

Leigh pushed the ignition button, and the powerful car hummed to life. She was about to turn on the wipers when Peyton laid her hand on her arm. Leigh felt her touch all the way down to her toes.

"Leigh."

Peyton's voice was quiet, and Leigh was afraid of what she was going to say. She decided to take the offensive. "It's not a problem, Peyton. You can't stand around waiting for a ride soaking wet. You're freezing. We'll be back before anyone even knows you're gone."

Leigh pulled into the driveway of the house Peyton pointed to and drove toward a two-car garage with a large RV bay to the left and an apartment above the garage. The entire structure looked professionally designed and built, the white trim a tasteful accent to the gray siding. A deck, complete with a white picket railing, spanned the top of two separate garage doors with two large French doors providing access to the deck. The peak of the roof was severe, and for a garage, the overall structure was stunning. Leigh parked in front of the white RV door.

"I'll just be a minute. Would you like to come in?" The rain had stopped in the few minutes it took to get to Peyton's place.

By the expression on Peyton's face, Leigh wasn't sure if she wanted her to or was just being polite. Suddenly, she had to know more about Peyton. "Sure."

The door leading to the stairs was on the side, and as they rounded the corner, Peyton said, "It's not much. My brother and his wife live here." She used her thumb like a hitchhiker to point to the house on their right.

Not much? This garage is almost nicer than my entire house, Leigh thought.

"Obviously you and your brother are close?" That was a big assumption on Leigh's part. Just because Peyton lived above his garage didn't mean they had dinner together every night and watched football on Sundays.

Peyton chuckled. "Yeah. Sometimes too close. He and his wife Olivia are always inviting me for dinner, or she brings me leftovers. Somewhere along the line he's forgotten I'm the big sister."

The affection Peyton had for her brother was obvious, and Leigh wondered if her indifferent feelings for her own brother were as evident to everyone. Bruce was twelve years older than her, and she had just started first grade when Bruce went away to college. They'd never been close. After he graduated, he moved to Paris, and she'd seen him only twice in the intervening years.

Peyton unlocked the door, opened it, and stepped to the side, indicating for her to enter first. A skylight overhead provided enough light that the narrow staircase felt much larger than it actually was.

The top of the landing was small, and Peyton reached around her to unlock a second door. Their bodies brushed, and Leigh felt Peyton freeze. Her jaw muscles were tight, the scar on her cheek prominent. Peyton slowly turned her head, their eyes locking. The small area suddenly grew much, much smaller.

Desire flared in Peyton's eyes and Leigh responded. Her breath stopped somewhere in the middle of her chest, her stomach tumbling somewhere farther south. Peyton's eyes dropped to her mouth. All Leigh needed to do was step into her arms.

Peyton shook her head and stepped back, what little distance she could, and opened the door. The moment gone, Leigh turned and went inside.

To her right was the bathroom, a small kitchenette with a bar and two stools to her left. In front of her was the living room, light spilling in through a pair of French doors. A recliner covered in a geometric pattern of blues sat to the left of a couch located under a large window, its shutters open. An enormous flat-screen television was mounted on the wall across from the couch. Colorful prints hung on the walls that were painted a pale blue, the trim and crown molding a bright white. Another door to her right probably led into the bedroom. The apartment was warm and inviting and impeccably neat.

"This is not much?" Leigh stepped farther inside, the carpet thick under her feet. "Peyton, this is beautiful."

"It's just a place to live," Peyton said solemnly. "I don't get too attached to stuff or things. Make yourself at home. I have water in the fridge, so help yourself. I'll just be a few minutes."

The entire apartment was probably no more than six hundred square feet yet, with the amount of light that streamed in, felt much larger. Leigh opened the small refrigerator door. A dozen bottles of water were lined up in neat rows on the top shelf, along with a gallon of milk and a container of Greek yogurt. Apples and several oranges sat on the second shelf, with something green in the salad crisper. Assorted bottles of ketchup, mustard, and salad dressing were in the door. Peyton definitely ate better than she did, with two take-out containers and a twelve pack of Michelob Ultra in her fridge.

Leigh heard the shower door close a little too hard, and her legs moved of their own accord toward it. Peyton hadn't locked the door, and it opened silently. Leigh stepped farther inside, the view in front of her breathtaking.

The shower was small, the clear doors giving Leigh an unobstructed view of Peyton's nakedness. Her hands pressed against the wall in front of her, and her head was bowed, water cascading over her shoulders, down her back, and gliding over her ass. She looked like a goddess. That was the only word that could even begin to describe how beautiful Peyton looked. Her muscles were tense, as if she was straining against some inner turmoil. Peyton turned her head and their eyes locked.

Leigh unbuttoned her shirt and let it drop to the floor. She unhooked the front closure of her bra, her breasts spilling out. Peyton's mouth fell open. Dropping her bra on the floor, Leigh toed off her shoes and unbuckled her pants, pulling them and her panties off in one movement.

Peyton's eyes followed her movements, heating Leigh's skin as if she were touching her. Desire burned low in Leigh's belly, anticipation tingling in her veins. She pulled the tie from her hair, slid the shower door open, and stepped in.

Peyton started to say something, and Leigh put her finger over her lips. "We are two consenting adults, and I don't care. If you do, you better say something now." Peyton smiled when Leigh didn't remove her fingers so she could speak, even if she wanted to. Obviously Leigh didn't want her to.

Peyton reached for her and their lips met, hot and searching, their breath mingling with the steam from the water. Leigh wrapped her arms around Peyton's neck, pulling her close. Peyton's kisses became impatient and insistent, and Leigh struggled to keep up with her demands. She needed to be closer to Peyton, inside her, and she raised herself on her toes and leaned into her.

The shower was small, and Peyton easily pinned her back against the smooth, cool surface. She moaned into Peyton's mouth when her hands started to roam. When they cupped her breasts, she was sure her knees would buckle. When Peyton pinched her nipples, Leigh arched into her, digging her nails into Peyton's neck.

It had been a long time since a woman had touched her. Longer still since she'd wanted someone as desperately as she wanted Peyton. Her primal need for Peyton to take her was shocking. Peyton's hand drifted down her stomach and slid into her. Awash in sensation, she dragged her lips from Peyton's, gasping for air. Leigh ran her hands up and down Peyton's back, and Peyton arched into her, nipples hard against her chest.

Leigh cupped her hand behind Peyton's neck and pulled her down for another kiss. She didn't know what aroused her more— Peyton's kisses, the feel of her breasts against hers, or Peyton's desire for her. She didn't try to figure it out; she didn't care.

Peyton pulled her hand away, and Leigh moaned her disappointment. Peyton kissed her neck.

"Not here, not like this, not again," Peyton said, her voice husky, her breathing shallow.

Putting both hands on her ass, Peyton lifted her, and Leigh wrapped her legs around her waist. She reached behind her, shut off the water, opened the door, and wrapped them both in a large, soft towel.

The distance to Peyton's bed was mercifully short, and in an instant, Leigh was lying on cool, crisp sheets, Peyton on top of her. Their kisses were feverish, almost frantic in their haste for each other. Leigh's head lay in the crook of Peyton's arm as she sucked on first one nipple, then the other. Leigh squirmed as Peyton's hand wandered across her stomach and over her hip. She wanted Peyton's fingers on her, in her, and when Peyton finally touched her, Leigh again found it hard to breathe.

Peyton leaned back, looking at Leigh's body as if memorizing every detail before it was taken away. "You are so beautiful," she whispered.

Leigh closed her eyes as Peyton stroked her, drowning in sensation.

"Look at me," Peyton said, her voice demanding.

Leigh's ears roared and her pulse skyrocketed with desire at the passion reflected in Peyton's eyes. She felt more beautiful and desired than she had in a long time. Peyton flicked her clit.

"Oh, God." Leigh could barely speak. Her breathing was too fast, and she was light-headed. She pulled Peyton back to her for another searing kiss. Their lips had barely touched when Peyton slid her fingers into her. Leigh's climax roared through her almost before she knew it was coming.

Her head started to clear, and Leigh knew Peyton was beside her. Her breathing was still coming quickly, but her ears were no longer ringing. She could feel Peyton's heart beating hard and fast, her own breath shallow.

Leigh rolled on top of Peyton and slid her thigh between her legs. Peyton moaned and pulled her closer. It was Leigh's turn to worship Peyton's body, and she took her time doing so. She slid her lips and tongue down Peyton's neck, enjoying the taste of her. She sucked on the throbbing pulse point, and Peyton tugged on her hair.

"Touch me," Peyton said breathlessly.

"Patience," Leigh whispered in her ear an instant before nipping her earlobe.

"I don't have any." Peyton tightened her legs around Leigh, rocking against her.

Leigh dropped her head and lightly bit one of Peyton's hard nipples. The stronger she sucked, the faster Peyton rocked against her. She slid her fingers between them, and Peyton gasped in pleasure, quickening her pace.

Leigh had to have more. She needed to feel Peyton's flesh around her fingers, feel it pulsate in orgasm. Leigh shifted, and her fingers found what she needed. She rubbed Peyton's clit with her thumb, and Peyton came in her hand.

"I love your tatt," Peyton said, commenting on the tattoo she was finally able to look at without fear of getting caught. It featured a woman on a motorcycle, her hair cascading out of her helmet.

They were in Peyton's bed, the ceiling fan cooling their heated bodies after hours of lovemaking.

"My mother practically killed me when she saw it. I was seventeen and used my sister's ID."

"Did your sister get in trouble?" Peyton warmed, thinking about Leigh doing something so naughty.

"No. She had no idea I took it. She was at the movies with her boyfriend, and I snagged it out of her purse. I thought my mom would have a stroke. Of course, by then it was too late, and she couldn't do anything about it. She grounded me until I was eighteen. Longest eight months of my life. I lost my girlfriend and spent the entire summer in the library."

"You had a girlfriend at seventeen?"

"Of course I did. I'd had several by then," Leigh said somewhat proudly. "How old were you when you had your first?"

"My first or my first girlfriend?"

"Is there a difference?"

"No. Fifteen."

"Fifteen? You were fifteen?" Leigh tried to wiggle out of Peyton's arms. Peyton pulled her tighter.

"Yes. I was fifteen. She was seventeen, and I was in love. Actually, it was simply lust, but I thought it was love at the time."

"What happened?"

"She graduated and went to Vassar."

"Vassar? The all-girl's college?"

"Yep. I'm sure she was like a kid in a toy store. Kim could be quite charming when she wanted to be."

"Vassar is a women's college, not a lesbian college."

"I know that, but Kim was determined to sleep her way through as many as she could."

"What happened to her? Did you two keep in touch?"

"No. She walked across the graduation stage that hot summer night and kept walking. She never looked back. I was devastated." Peyton put her hand over her heart dramatically. "She took my virtue, my innocence, and my belief in happily-ever-after."

"You seem to have recovered nicely," Leigh said when it was obvious Peyton was joking.

"I did, didn't I? You can thank Kim for that thing I did to you earlier. The one when you begged me not to stop."

Leigh's pulse started racing, and her stomach flipped at the memory. She rolled on top of Peyton. "Remind me again exactly what that was."

Peyton's eyes turned dark, and she did as she was told.

CHAPTER TWENTY-FIVE

Peyton sat in front of the driveway of a modest ranch with a neatly trimmed front yard complete with a few trees and a blooming flowerbed adjacent to the front door. She glanced at the clock on the dash. Leigh was fifteen minutes late from the time Peyton had told her she'd pick her up for dinner. She looked up as Leigh's truck turned into the drive and pulled into the garage. Her motocross bike was secured in the bed. Leigh got out of the driver's side and hurried over to Peyton's truck.

"I'm so sorry," Leigh said quickly. She was still in her riding clothes, her face smeared with dirt, her hair a mess.

Peyton thought she looked nothing short of beautiful, just like she had lying naked in her bed a few days ago.

"One of the guys took a spill, and we had to get his gear packed up."

"Is he okay?" Peyton asked, opening her own door and getting out.

"He'll be okay. He banged up his shoulder so he was pretty worthless. Come in. I'll take a quick shower and just be a minute."

Peyton followed Leigh through a neat, clean garage and quickly found herself inside a brightly lit foyer.

"The living room is straight ahead, the kitchen, through there." Leigh pointed to their left. "Help yourself to anything and make yourself at home."

Their eyes locked, sharing the memory of what came after Peyton had said the same words. "I'll be just a minute."

The living room was a splash of color, with a red leather couch, a navy side chair, and two walls painted a bold shade of green. The shutters were bright white. No magazines lay on the coffee table; instead were three file folders with labels containing a variety of acronyms she didn't understand. She passed through to the kitchen and, along with a few dishes in the sink, found equal amounts of color. Leigh's house was comfortable and lived in. It breathed life.

Peyton wandered past the kitchen into a small dining room and an office with a laptop and a very large monitor. Several books and a few papers were strewn across a large wooden desk.

Peyton returned to the living room, passing the door that Leigh had disappeared through earlier. The door hadn't fully latched and had swung open. Peyton took a few tentative steps forward, stopping in the doorway to Leigh's bedroom. The bed wasn't made, one side still neatly tucked, pillows in place. A shaft of jealousy shot through Peyton as she thought of someone else on the other side, the covers a tangled mess.

She turned at movement she caught out of the corner of her eye. Leigh stood there in nothing but a very, very short yellow towel, another wrapped around her head.

A thousand thoughts raced through her mind. Leigh was three steps away, more skin showing than covered. Leigh was looking at her with an intensity both exhilarating and frightening. Fraternization was frowned upon at the club. Marcus had gone out on a limb for her by giving her a job. She couldn't throw away Marcus's trust and her integrity for a quick tumble in the sheets, but then again she already had.

She wanted Leigh, more than she'd wanted anyone before. She was smart, quick-witted, and laughed easily. She was absolutely stunning and took her breath away. She had to have her, touch every inch of her skin, feel every muscle tighten and twitch under her fingers, taste her.

Peyton didn't question her visceral reaction to Leigh; it was too much to think about. She had never wanted anyone as much as she wanted Leigh, and for once, she refused to stop and analyze her desire. Before she could utter any protest, Leigh dropped her towel and walked toward her, unwinding the towel from her wet hair and dropping that too onto the floor. She didn't stop until she wrapped her arms around Peyton's neck and pulled her into a searing kiss.

Just as before, Leigh's kiss instantly turned explosive. Her mouth was hot, her tongue demanding access to explore. Peyton's arms instinctively wrapped around Leigh and started their own exploration of her soft skin. After several moments, Leigh shifted her attention to Peyton's neck.

Peyton felt the cool air brush against her back as Leigh unbuttoned her shirt and pulled her undershirt over her head. The sensation of Leigh's hands on her was overwhelming.

"God, you feel good," Leigh said, her warm breath caressing Peyton's neck.

The words made her nipples tight, the huskiness causing shivers to dance across her skin. Desperate for something to steady her, Peyton held on to Leigh's hips.

Leigh squeezed her nipples, and Peyton arched her back. Leigh alternatively nipped and kissed at the sensitive skin on her breasts. When she took her nipple into her mouth, Peyton thought her knees would buckle.

"I can't stand up much longer if you keep doing that."

"You are so beautiful," Leigh said, mumbling against her breast.

Peyton ran her hands through Leigh's hair, gripping it to hold her mouth right where it was. She felt agony and ecstasy simultaneously and didn't want this tantalizing woman to stop.

"Leigh," she said, swaying on her feet.

Leith took her hand and led her the few steps to the bed. She pulled down the comforter and sheets in one motion, and suddenly Leigh was on top of her.

Peyton's body heated everywhere Leigh touched her, and the throbbing between her legs pounded for release. Leigh's hands and mouth explored every inch of her, and Peyton silently begged for release. It had been a long time since she'd given someone such free access to her. Peyton wanted Leigh everywhere, wanted to feel the pressure of her fingers, the skipping of her fingers over her skin, her hot mouth on her again. She wanted to feel Leigh's weight on her, her arms and legs wrapped around her, holding her tight as she came. And she wanted, no, needed to come hard, to lose control, to lose herself. To see nothing but stars and the woman on top of her. She wanted to forget where she was, what day it was, and what was waiting for her. She wanted to feel completely alive again. Peyton needed to feel nothing but Leigh inside her, taking her to that place where nothing else mattered but nerve endings alive with pleasure.

When she couldn't take it anymore she said, "Leigh, touch me. Please."

Peyton had no more pride, no inhibition, no strength. She needed this. Needed Leigh like she had never needed anyone before. She needed to release herself in the safety of Leigh's arms.

"Look at me. Peyton, look at me."

Leigh's voice penetrated the overwhelming haze of desire and sensation. The instant Leigh touched her, Peyton exploded, her body awash in pleasure. Higher and higher she climbed until suddenly there was nothing.

"How did you get this?" Leigh lightly traced the scar on her face. Instead of the question embarrassing her and making her try to hide it, Leigh's touch soothed her. It was dark, but the light coming in from Leigh's window was enough to see by.

"A minor skirmish" was all she said. No way was she going to tell Leigh that one of her fellow inmates hadn't liked the way she looked at her and had come after Peyton with a shank.

"Looks a little more than *minor* to me." Leigh kissed her cheek, tracing the line with her mouth.

"No plastic surgeons on call that night," Peyton said sarcastically. She'd stopped lamenting the inferior treatment of her cut years ago and didn't want this line of questioning to go much further.

"And this?" Leigh asked, picking up her hand and kissing the misshapen pinkie on her left hand.

"Same skirmish."

"Hmm," Leigh mumbled, licking Peyton's finger sensually.

"Remind me never to get in a skirmish with you."

The beginnings of arousal kicked in again. Had it ever gone away? "You make it feel better when you do that." She moved her legs back and forth restlessly on the sheet.

"Hmm," Leigh said again, sliding Peyton's finger slowly out of her mouth. "Any other injuries you'd like me to kiss and make you feel better?"

Leigh's eyes were hot with desire and sparkling with mischief. Peyton had a hard time forming a sentence.

"Kim did break my heart," Peyton said, catching on.

Leigh slowly kissed and licked a trail up Peyton's arm, across her shoulder and collarbone, and down her chest, finding just the right spot where her heart had been broken years ago.

Leigh's mouth was warm and wet, her teeth nipping her breast and nipple. Peyton grabbed her hair, holding her head in place until she almost couldn't stand it anymore.

"I had my appendix out."

"Yes, you did. I saw that," Leigh said, shifting her attention farther south. "How old were you?"

"Six."

Leigh stopped kissing her and looked up. "Six?"

"It hurt. I was a kid," Peyton said, a slight pout on her lips.

Leigh kissed the very, very faint scar and said, "You poor baby in that big, scary hospital bed."

"I have cramps once in a while."

Leigh laughed. "Now?"

"No. Not now," Peyton said quickly, afraid Leigh would stop. "But sometimes." She tried to look convincing. She'd never had more than a twinge or two during her period.

"The curse of being a..." Leigh hesitated just above Peyton's pubic bone. "A woman." She lowered her head and placed her lips right where Peyton needed them.

"God, that feels good." Peyton's mind had turned to mush minutes ago, and she couldn't think of another, more descriptive word to describe the way Leigh made her body sing.

"Feels pretty good on this end too," Leigh said before going back to work soothing all of Peyton's aches and pains.

CHAPTER TWENTY-SIX

"S he what?"

Peyton sat up so quickly, Leigh almost tumbled to the floor. They were lying on Peyton's couch, limbs still tangled from their almost unquenchable desire for each other. Leigh had stopped by to pick up Peyton to take her to dinner a few nights later, and one thing had quickly led to another, as it always did when they were together. This time they had made it only as far as the couch before they were naked.

"Where is she?" Peyton asked, frantically looking for her clothes. Leigh got up and helped her. She had no idea who was on the other end or what "she" had done, but Peyton was obviously upset.

"I'll be right there." Peyton hung up the phone and stepped into her shorts. "I'm sorry. I've got to go."

"Is everything okay?" Leigh asked when Peyton didn't give any further explanation. It was obvious she wasn't planning to, but Leigh was curious as to what had caused such a reaction.

"It will be." Peyton didn't say any more as she pulled her shirt over her head and stuffed her feet into her shoes. She stuck her socks in her pocket and headed toward the door.

Leigh was shocked at her abrupt departure and bent to pick up her own clothes.

Peyton stopped before she got to the door, turned, and hurried back to her. "I'm sorry I've got to go," she said, a little calmer than she had the first time she said it. "I'll call you later, okay? Lock up when you leave. No hurry." She quickly kissed Leigh, spun around, and went out the front door.

Leigh heard Peyton's tires squeal as she backed out of her driveway, leaving Leigh alone in Peyton's apartment. Her skin still tingled where Peyton had touched her, still hummed with contentment. Her limbs were loose, her mind clear. Good sex really did clear your head, she thought. She knew she should leave, but an overwhelming opportunity to learn more about Peyton overruled propriety.

Leigh wandered around the apartment, touching a few things but making note of everything. One of the initial things Leigh noticed the first time she was here was the abundance of color. The walls were painted varying shades of bold colors, the furniture fabric and draperies the same. She'd been too busy envisioning Peyton naked in the shower to pay much attention to the decor.

Large, abstract paintings covered the walls, mixed in with framed photographs. Leigh stepped closer and saw recent pictures of Peyton with an older couple, all three beaming for the camera. She picked up a frame showing Peyton with Marcus and another woman. A flash of jealousy shot through Leigh, and she quickly put the picture back in its place.

Peyton had an eclectic array of books on the shelves that ran floor to ceiling on the far wall. A quick glance identified the latest best sellers from several popular, main-stream authors, at least a dozen biographies, and more than a handful of nonfiction books about the Civil War and World War I. But it was the thin books that caught her eyes.

Leigh ran her fingers over the well-worn spines, recognizing the titles of some of her favorite lesbian fiction. Forrest, Kallmaker, Carr, Fletcher, Taite, Radclyffe, and many more were lined up neatly according to author. Every genre was accounted for, and Leigh was more than a little impressed. She pulled one out and opened the cover.

A newspaper clipping fell out and floated to the floor. Leigh picked it up and saw a photo of a much younger Peyton in a tuxedo, smiling and holding an enormous trophy. Leigh's ever-present arousal when she thought of Peyton kicked up a notch. Standing in her living room completely naked was slightly naughty and sensuous and added to her arousal. She read the headline under the picture:

PEYTON BROADER DOES IT AGAIN!
Peyton Broader, 20, won her third consecutive NCAA golfer of the year title last night in a star-studded gala hosted by ESPN. The black-tie event was held at the posh Julian Hotel in New York, and over three hundred of the nation's finest men and women collegiate athletes were in attendance.

Leigh read the rest of the short article and placed it back inside the book. She must have been using it as a bookmark, the age of the article and the book an indication. She put the book back in its spot on the shelf. A warmth flowed through her veins as she looked around the small, neat room. This is where Peyton lived, where she slept, watched television, and ate breakfast. She pictured Peyton doing everyday mundane tasks like folding clothes, taking out the garbage, packing her lunch, and opening her mail.

What did she look like first thing in the morning? Was she a grouch until she had coffee, or did she rise early and energized? Was she *Good Morning America* or *The Today Show*? CNN, FOX, or CNBC? Did she watch *Scandal*, the History Channel, or National Geographic? Was she handy with a hammer? Have a green thumb, feed the birds? Did she use paper or plastic? Butter or margarine? Wash her whites in hot or the economical cold water? Did she want a dog? A cat? Kids?

"Whoa, Leigh," she said out loud. "Do not go there." She repeated those four words several times as she got dressed and locked the door behind her.

CHAPTER TWENTY-SEVEN

"Where is she?" Peyton asked her mother after she passed the security desk in the emergency room. It had taken her twelve minutes to get across town to the hospital where her sister had been admitted.

"She's in the back. The doctor is with her."

Maria looked exhausted and worried, as any mother would when her child was found unresponsive on the bathroom floor.

"Can't you go back there? See what's going on?"

"This isn't my hospital," Maria said, grasping Peyton's hand and pulling her into the chair beside her. "I don't have privileges here, and I don't know anyone. I'm just another family member relegated to the waiting room."

Peyton wanted to pace, but her mother had a firm grasp of her hand and didn't let go. Peyton wondered if that was for her benefit or her mother's.

"What happened?"

"I hadn't heard from Elizabeth in several weeks and decided to go over there and give her a piece of my mind." Maria's face was angry, then went pale. "I knocked on the door, and when she didn't answer, I tried the knob. It was unlocked, and I found her in the bathroom. She was unconscious and I couldn't rouse her. I called 911, and here we are."

"Jesus," Peyton said, running her free hand over her face. "Jesus," she said again when she realized it smelled like Leigh. She wiped it on her shorts. "Do you have any idea?"

"Do you mean did I see any evidence of drugs? I'm not stupid, Peyton," she said in response to Peyton's surprise. "I know your sister drinks too much and takes drugs, but she is an adult, and I can do little to stop her. No. I didn't see anything in the bathroom, but I'm not sure about the rest of the apartment. It was filthy, and I didn't really notice. I was looking for her when I came in and following the stretcher on the way out." Peyton's mother's voice cracked on the last few words.

"Where are Dad and Marcus? And Natalie?"

"Your father's out of town and is catching the next flight. Marcus and Olivia are on their way. They were in Prescott when I called. Natalie's in New Mexico for a case. She asked that you let her know what's happening after we find out."

"Family of Elizabeth Broader?" An African-American male in dark-blue scrubs, looking quite grim, stood in an open doorway. Peyton and her mother stood up simultaneously.

"I'm her sister and this is our mother," Peyton said. She felt her mother tremble beside her. Peyton put her arm through her mother's to steady her. "How is Lizzy?" Peyton asked, falling back on her childhood name.

"Come with me," he said, opening the door wider. "I'll take you back. The doctor will talk with you in a minute."

The man led them down a hall with individual treatment areas partitioned off with dull-gray curtains. Several of the beds were empty, and Peyton saw legs under the curtains of a few others. The open area shifted into a series of glassed rooms, four on each side. The man stopped just outside the third room on the left.

A short, round woman exited the room, closing the door behind her. "I'm Doctor Harris. I've been taking care of Elizabeth."

Peyton and her mother introduced themselves. Peyton's heart was racing. All indications were that her sister was not okay.

"Can you give me her history?" the doctor asked, and her mother quickly and efficiently filled her in. Peyton was shocked at the length and severity of her sister's addiction.

"She came in unresponsive, with very low blood pressure. We drew some blood, ran some tests, and the preliminary results show high levels of cocaine and alcohol, a very dangerous combination."

Anger replaced worry as Peyton realized just how stupid and careless Elizabeth had become.

"Is she okay?" she heard her mother ask.

"Yes, for now. We gave her some Narcan and pumped her stomach, just a precaution. She's resting."

"Narcan is used to counteract the effect of most drugs," her mother explained to her.

"I'd like to keep her overnight. She was pretty sick when she came in. I'd also like for a social worker and a substance-abuse counselor to talk to her when she wakes up. We can recommend a treatment program, if that's what she wants."

"Of course," Maria said, nodding her agreement. "Can we see her?"

"For a few minutes. Then they'll take her upstairs." The doctor stepped away from the door.

Peyton held her mother's hand as they approached Elizabeth's bed. She was hooked up to assorted monitors and had several tubes running into an IV in her right arm. Maria looked at everything, including the labels on the bags hanging on the IV stand, with a practiced clinical eye. She must have approved, because she nodded as if in agreement with the medication for her daughter.

Maria went to Elizabeth first, Peyton to the other side of the bed. Her little sister looked small and frail, with dark circles under her eyes. She looked like she'd aged a few years since she'd seen her last. She was rail-thin, the need for the drugs obviously outweighing her need for food.

"She went to therapy after, but I don't think she listened." Maria said, surprising Peyton.

Peyton knew what the "after" was referencing.

"After the initial shock, she acted like nothing had happened, and we all knew that wasn't healthy. We took her to a therapist, for several months then and when you were in Nelson. The doctor kept reporting that she just sat there, wouldn't talk about anything, wouldn't answer their questions, nothing. We took her to somebody else, and it was the same. After the third one, we didn't know what to do, so we had her admitted to a residential treatment facility."

"What? Why didn't you tell me?" Peyton asked, angry at her mother for keeping something so important from her.

"There was nothing you could do, Peyton. You didn't need anything else to worry about."

Peyton calmed down; her mother was right. She would have gone nuts with worry as she struggled every day to survive.

"Did it help?" Peyton knew the answer to her question.

"No. After four months we brought her home. No one could do anything, and I couldn't stand for her to be in a strange place. Maybe we should have kept her there longer. Maybe they could have gotten through to her. Maybe…"

Peyton hurried around the bed and held her mother as she cried.

CHAPTER TWENTY-EIGHT

I'm sorry I ran out on you the other night." Peyton had called earlier, and they'd agreed to meet at Leigh's house after work. She needed to see Leigh, to set her life back on track again. She needed to feel alive, a connection, to disappear into the abyss of pleasure. Peyton started to explain but lost track of reality when Leigh pulled her into her arms and kissed her before her front door closed.

"Is everything all right? You were obviously upset." Leigh snuggled into Peyton, their legs intertwined, bodies close.

"My sister, Elizabeth. Her life has spiraled out of control. She overdosed the other night. We don't know if it was intentional or an accident."

"Oh, Peyton, I'm so sorry." Leigh shifted, resting her weight on her elbows so she could see Peyton better. "How is she?"

"Physically, she's fine. We're trying to convince her she needs to get some help." Peyton didn't want to think about the ugly scene this morning. Elizabeth would need extensive therapy to deal with not only her addiction, but why she needed to hide behind drugs and alcohol to get through every day. Peyton had had no escape and had been forced to face her demons every second of every day. She'd risked everything for Elizabeth and had paid her dues.

As much as she tried to put them away, in a place where they no longer mattered, no longer dominated her life, now they were once again front and center.

"How old is she?"

"She'll be twenty in a few weeks."

"Wow, that's tough. Are you two close?"

"We used to be."

"What happened?" Peyton immediately tensed and got out of bed, looking around for her clothes. Leigh had struck a nerve, obviously a very raw one.

"I don't mean to pry," Leigh said, pulling on a robe hanging from the back of the bedroom door.

"I've gotta go." Peyton picked up her shoes and passed Leigh. The scene was eerily reminiscent of the one they were just talking about, except this time she was running away, not running to. She heard Leigh call her name before she closed the door behind her.

Peyton threw her truck into gear, tires squealing as they slipped over the asphalt. She had to leave, had to get out of there before she suffocated under the weight of her secret. Peyton knew the day would come when she would have to make a decision. Did she tell Leigh what had happened and hope she understood, or did she simply move on? Surely, by now, she knew. She'd probably Googled her again before her first lesson.

❖

"You just left?"

"Worse," Peyton said, barely able to make eye contact with Lori. "I practically ran out of her house."

"You haven't told her." It wasn't a question.

"No."

"Why not?"

Lori was nothing but blunt, and most of the time Peyton loved her for it. This, however, was not one of those times. "I've asked myself that question a thousand times."

"And what's your answer?"

Peyton knew she had no choice but to answer. "I like her."

Lori looked at her, expecting more, but she didn't have any other explanation.

"Okay…" she finally said when Peyton didn't offer more.

"I like her."

"You said that. That's pretty clear." Lori set her fork down, giving Peyton her full attention. Lori had had to threaten Peyton to get her to meet for lunch at the Wildflower Cafe. "What's going on, Peyton? Don't bullshit me or give me some tough prison-girl crap."

"I don't want to tell her," Peyton said pitifully. Like if she didn't bring it up it never happened.

"I don't think you have a choice. Unless this is just a hookup."

Peyton had thought it was just that. At least it had started out that way. Leigh was a passionate, aggressive, demanding lover, and Peyton couldn't get enough of her. Every time they were together, it was better than the time before. She was barely back in her clothes before she was thinking about the next time.

She'd spent weeks rationalizing the situation as making up for lost time. She'd fully intended to let it run its course, and when things looked like they were going to the next level, she'd quietly drift away. But somewhere between "Beverage, ladies?" and last night, it had shifted without her knowing it. Now, she didn't want to stop seeing Leigh.

"What's going on in that head of yours, Peyton? You know I'm in your corner whatever you do."

Lori had been there for Peyton, and she was the only one Peyton trusted to tell her the truth.

"I think I've fallen for her."

"Peyton…"

"I know. It's too soon. I just got out. I don't have my life together yet. I'm under the thumb of my parole officer, and my life isn't my own and won't be for months."

"That's not what I was going to say." Lori reached across the table as far as she could, her pregnant belly making it a long reach, and put her hands over Peyton's.

"I think she's good for you, and I haven't even met her. You're smiling more, your face glows, and you just look…I don't know, happy. You may not want my opinion, but…"

"That never stopped you before," Peyton said, the tension lifting from her chest.

"And have I ever been wrong? No, I have not," Lori said before Peyton had a chance to answer. "I think you should tell her. She probably already knows, and you can't not talk about it. It's kind of like how everyone on the team knew you were a lesbian before you even told us. We were afraid to bring it up. Maybe she's afraid to ask."

Several moments passed while Peyton reflected on her revelation that she had, indeed, fallen for Leigh. She tossed the thoughts around in her head, and they tumbled back to the same place. She was crazy about Leigh.

"How does she feel?" Lori asked.

"I'm not sure. She hasn't said or done anything to lead me to believe one way or the other."

"Why do you think that is?"

Peyton shrugged, her only answer.

"Is she seeing anyone else?"

"I don't think so."

"Do you want her to?"

The mere thought of another woman kissing Leigh, touching her, making her sigh with pleasure, call her name in the dark made Peyton's stomach turn and her blood boil.

"No."

"Then maybe that's where you start. Tell her you're not seeing anyone else and you'd like the same commitment from her. If she agrees, then it's clear that she thinks your time together is more than a booty call. If she says no, or dances around it, then that's your answer. Either way, you know where you stand. But you need to tell her if you want to have any relationship with her."

CHAPTER TWENTY-NINE

"Peyton," Leigh said, pushing her head from between her legs. "Peyton!"

"What? What's the matter? Did I hurt you?"

"Someone's pounding on your door."

Peyton heard it then. Three solid knocks. She looked up the expanse of Leigh's body to the clock on the nightstand. Two twelve. Another three pounds. "Fuck!" It could only be one person. This was their third night together at her apartment, and she'd grown complacent with letting Leigh stay the night.

Peyton scrambled out of bed, pulled on a pair of jeans and a T-shirt, and ran her fingers through her short hair. She turned on the light.

"Get dressed," she said, gritting her teeth in anger.

"What?"

"Get dressed, now." The last thing she wanted was for Conway to find Leigh naked in her bed.

"Fuck, fuck, fuck," Peyton said, crossing the room to her front door, turning her lights on along the way. She picked up her cell phone and activated the cameras.

"Who is it?" she asked, even though she looked through the peephole and saw it was Conway.

"Your fairy godmother," he said, his tone sleazy,

Peyton opened the door.

"Good morning, sunshine," Conway said brushing past her way too closely. "What took you so long? Were you otherwise *occupado?*" he asked stupidly in his equally insulting attempt at Spanish. He looked around the room.

"It's the middle of the night."

"Uh-huh. You alone? Get lucky tonight?"

"Why do you always ask me that?"

"Because it's my job to know who you're hanging around with." His tone was belligerent.

Just then her bedroom door opened, and Conway's head whipped around so fast, Peyton wouldn't have been surprised if he got whiplash.

"Well, well, well. Look who we have here." If voices could leer, Conway's would be doing it.

Leigh looked from Peyton, to Conway, and back to Peyton again, her expression unreadable. She had her phone in her hand.

"Who are you?" Leigh asked.

"I'm asking the questions here, honey. Who are you?"

"I don't need to tell you that, and I'm not your honey. As far as I can tell this is a home invasion, and I've got 9 and 1 pushed on my phone, and my thumb on the other 1. So, unless you want the cops here, you'd better tell me who you are."

"Hang up that phone, sister," Conway said menacingly.

"I'm not your sister. Yes, hello," Leigh said into the phone a moment later. "There's a man in the living room that I don't recognize. Would you please send an officer right away? Peyton, what's your address?"

Peyton looked at Leigh, stunned, her reaction on Conway. He reached into his back pocket, and Peyton could swear she saw steam coming out of his hairy ears.

"That had better be your wallet you're reaching for. Yes," she said to the 9-1-1 operator. "The man is about six feet and probably weighs two eighty," Leigh said into her phone. "He has on blue jeans, a black pullover with NAVY across the front, and dirty white tennis shoes. He has short black hair and a Fu-Manchu mustache."

"Leigh, it's all right."

"There's no need to call the cops, honey. I'm Manny Conway. Peyton's parole officer."

"He says he's a parole office. He's reaching into his back pocket. Hand it to her," Leigh said when he pulled out his wallet.

Peyton saw Conway's anger notch up six or ten points on the blow-a-gasket scale. He tossed his wallet at her feet. She didn't pick it up. No way was she going to touch it.

"Leigh, it's okay. We don't need the police."

Leigh never took her eyes off Conway and several seconds later said into the phone, "Everything's cleared up. We don't need an officer." Leigh gave the dispatcher her name and address, and after a few more reassurances, Leigh hung up and put her phone in the pocket of her jeans.

"Just what in the fuck was all that about?" Conway barked at Peyton.

"You woke us up in the middle of the night. She didn't know who you were." Peyton knew trouble was coming.

"Do you know your girlfriend is an ex-con? A murderer?" Conway said to Leigh.

Leigh didn't answer, the shocked look on her face obvious she didn't.

"Hmm." Conway's sleazy eyes slid over Leigh's body. "Didn't know she was a bad girl? Oh, yeah, she was very bad." Conway laughed, but it sounded more like a bark. "Do you come here often?"

"Do you?"

"I said I'm asking the questions, doll."

"And I said I'm not your doll or your honey. If you want an answer, you ask me respectfully."

"My, my, Peyton. She's a spitfire. I'll bet that's exciting," he added, his eyes roaming over Leigh's body.

Peyton's anger rose even higher. "All right, Conway. You're here. Do your thing and leave."

"I think maybe we'll just sit and chat for a while," he said, settling his large girth onto the couch. "That is if you're done sitting on her face."

"That's enough!" Peyton said, raising her voice. "You come in here and give me your shit, not to the people that are here. She's leaving."

"She's not leaving until I say she's leaving," Conway said menacingly. "While your girlfriend's here," he said, tossing something to Peyton, "piss in the cup."

"What?" Peyton said, instinctively catching the sterile urine container.

"I'm sure she's seen your girl parts. Let's see what kind of party ya'll got going on."

Rage boiled inside Peyton. She never thought she could kill again, but right now she wasn't so sure.

"You know the drill," Conway said, not taking his eyes off Leigh.

"Yes, I do, and it does not include doing it in front of you." She was required to have an observed uranalysis, but only at an authorized facility.

"You are subject to random drug tests wherever and whenever I choose. And I choose now. And while we're at it, blow," he said, holding out the portable breathalyzer. "What's a party without a little brew?"

Peyton had never been so enraged and humiliated in her life. Conway was a prick. That was a given. She'd always wondered how far he'd go, and she doubted this was it.

"Leigh, you need to go." Peyton struggled to keep her anger in check.

"Peyton—"

"He has no reason or authority to keep you. Please go."

Leigh gave Conway a long, hard look before doing the same to Peyton. Peyton couldn't meet her eyes, humiliated that Leigh had seen this. Leigh walked by Peyton, touching her arm as she did. Peyton heard the door close behind her.

"She's quite a looker, Broader."

Peyton didn't comment. She refused to engage him in conversation, and certainly not about Leigh.

"I think you've got something on your chin there," he said, rubbing his own with his middle finger.

Peyton resisted the temptation to put her hands to her face. Knowing Conway, it was a ruse to rattle her. "All right. You've had your fun, and at my expense, Conway. Now trash my house and leave."

Conway stood up. "Not till I see you piss."

There was absolutely no way Peyton would degrade herself even more in front of this man. She didn't care about the consequences, so she just stood there and stared at him.

Long moments later she was still standing in the same place, her eyes never leaving his. Conway, however, had looked away first and was starting to squirm. Peyton knew she'd won. But at what cost?

Peyton tossed the container to the floor at his feet. She saw the little wheels turn in his head and wondered what his plan was to get out of this standoff he'd gotten them into.

"You bitch," Conway snarled before hurling himself at Peyton, driving her into the wall, his big body knocking the breath out of her. He flipped her over on her stomach and handcuffed her wrists so tight she had to bite her lip from crying out in pain. He grabbed them and pulled her to her feet, the angle of her arms behind her almost dislocating her shoulder. He spun her around, and when she saw the look in his eyes, Peyton knew he wasn't finished with her.

Conway's fist connected with her cheek, and Peyton staggered backward. He hit her again, and Peyton felt her cheek spilt under the force. She fell into the chair, blinking a few times to clear her head. For a fat slob, Conway packed a powerful punch. But in her defenseless position it wasn't difficult.

As he loomed over her, the excitement in his eyes frightened her. He grabbed the front of her shirt with both hands and pulled her up.

"We'll add resisting arrest," he said, and punched her in the stomach.

Peyton buckled to the floor.

CHAPTER THIRTY

Leigh was stunned. She was sitting in her car trying to make sense of what had just happened. Peyton had a parole officer? She knew what that meant. But what the fuck for? She had no experience with this type of situation, no idea what rights parole officers had and what Peyton was required to do. She was still trying to wrap her head around the fact that Peyton was a convicted felon.

A shaft of pain stabbed her as she recalled the look on Peyton's face when he had tossed the urinalysis cup at her. Peyton had told her to go home, but she couldn't. She definitely couldn't go back inside. That would be like throwing gas on a fire. Leigh decided to wait until he left, then go back and check on Peyton.

She didn't have her watch, but her phone was in the back pocket of her pants. She scrolled to her Sent calls and saw that only five minutes had passed since she called the police, and she had no idea how long he'd be up there or how long she should wait.

Peyton's front door opened, a shaft of light spilling out into the dark night. Leigh instinctively slid down in the seat so as not to be seen, which was ridiculous because her car was parked beside Peyton's truck.

Peyton stepped out, the man behind her. When he closed the door, he took all the light with him. Leigh couldn't be sure, but it looked like Peyton's hands were handcuffed behind her back. Could he do that? What had she done to warrant being treated that way?

Leigh had no idea. All she knew about the judicial system was what she saw on *Law and Order*, and even she was aware that justice wasn't served up in a tidy little bow in sixty minutes. Peyton stumbled, and the man yanked her to her feet by her hands. Leigh's simmering anger turned into rage. Peyton was unsteady on her feet as the man practically threw her into the backseat of his car. He hurried around to the driver's side and drove off.

Leigh didn't know what to do. Should she follow him? Where would he take Peyton? To his office, the police station, or some secluded place? It would be ridiculous to follow him. She knew nothing about how to do that. The headlights from her car would be a dead giveaway that she was behind them.

She couldn't get involved in this. Peyton was...was what? It wasn't like they were together. She didn't need this kind of complication in her life. The last thing she needed was to have her name linked to a convicted felon.

Leigh pulled up Google on her phone and typed in Peyton's name. The first two articles were ones she had read before, but the third caught her attention.

NCAA PLAYER OF THE YEAR SENTENCED TO FIFTEEN YEARS

Peyton Broader, twenty-two, three-time NCAA golfer of the year and LPGA rookie phenom, was sentenced today to fifteen years in Nelson Correctional Institute for Women for the murder of Norman Chandler.

Broader, after lengthy discussions with the district attorney determined to make an example of her, pleaded guilty to voluntary manslaughter for the May third shooting of Chandler in his front yard. Chandler, age 64, residing in the eighty-two hundred block of Thomas Street, had been arrested and charged with the kidnapping and sexual assault of a nine-year-old girl. Privacy rights of the victim prohibit The Republic from disclosing the victim's name; however, sources to the case told The Republic that Chandler's victim was Broader's younger sister.

Allegedly, Chandler grabbed the victim on her way home from school on a bright, sunny day and held her in an undisclosed location for three days until she managed to escape. Investigators confiscated a videotape of the alleged assault, with Chandler and the victim clearly visible, leaving little doubt of a jury guilty verdict.

Broader, however, took justice into her own hands late the evening of May third, confronting Chandler as he stepped out his front door. Neighbors said they heard what sounded like a shot but, when they looked out their windows, didn't see anything unusual.

Detective Ruth Smallsreed, of the Phoenix Police Department Homicide Squad, stated that, "After a brief investigation, it became clear that Peyton Christine Broader pulled the trigger. She was arrested at her home on May fourth at 10:30 am on suspicion of murder in the first degree. Broader offered no resistance when she was taken into custody."

When reached for comment, Chandler's family continued to deny that he had any involvement in the alleged kidnapping and assault on the nine-year-old girl. They stated he was home with them watching television when the alleged assault occurred. Attempts to contact Peyton Broader or other members of the Broader family went unanswered. Broader was immediately taken into custody and will serve her sentence at the Nelson Correctional Institute for Women.

Leigh flopped back into her chair, stunned. "Holy fuck." She enlarged the picture to the right of the article. It was definitely Peyton, albeit much younger.

A fourth link led Leigh to a very liberal, free newspaper.

The police department is tight-lipped about this case, as is the district attorney's office, but it doesn't take a rocket scientist to put the pieces together. Allegedly, and this reporter uses this term loosely, Chandler assaulted Broader's little sister, and she took it upon herself to be judge, jury, and executioner. As a result, Peyton Broader is trading her mortarboard and white doctor's coat for prison gray. Another promising life wasted.

Leigh clicked on several more articles detailing the media storm of Peyton's arrest. Supporters on either side were very vocal in their support for Peyton, and thousands of names on a petition to drop all charges were submitted to the district attorney's office. Another group, much more radical, picketed her parents' house and the courthouse for weeks after her arrest. Both sides were out again in full force the day of her sentencing.

"Holy Jesus." Leigh's heart raced. *I'm her parole officer.* The words kept echoing in her head as she sat in her car trying to wrap her thoughts around what she'd just found out. Peyton had killed someone. Leigh did the math. Peyton had spent nine years in prison.

The revelation stunned Leigh. She had no idea. Peyton hadn't given any indication. Did you tell someone you'd committed murder before you had sex with them? Like if you had an STD? Leigh felt used. How long would Peyton have continued to hide her history from her? How many more times would she kiss Leigh, touch her, make love to her?

"Oh my God," Leigh said, running her hand over her mouth, panic pushing all other emotions aside. *What if I caught something from her?* How in the hell had this happened? How had she missed the signs that Peyton was...was what? A loser?

A thousand awful thoughts raced through Leigh's mind as she drove home. Emotionally and physically exhausted, she hardly paid any attention to the route to her house. She stumbled from the garage into her home, her hands shaking so badly she could barely unlock the door. She stepped inside, threw the deadbolt behind her, and slid to the floor.

CHAPTER THIRTY-ONE

S omeone was stomping on her head. Or at least that's what it felt like, judging by the pounding behind her eyelids. Peyton opened her eye, blinked several times, but only the vision in her right eye was clear. She blinked a few more times before she figured out her left eye was swollen shut. She tentatively reached up and verified it was and felt stitches on her left cheekbone.

She tried to sit up, groaning at the pain in her stomach. With her good eye, she looked around and saw she was in a holding cell. The three other women there were looking at her curiously.

"I hope you gave him as good as you got," one of the ladies said, indicating her battered face.

"What time is it?" Peyton asked no one in particular. Her throat was raw.

"It's still before seven. They haven't brought breakfast in yet."

Peyton's stomach rolled, the thought of food nauseating. Holding her head, she leaned against the wall, drawing her feet under her.

She didn't remember much after Conway had tossed her into the backseat of his car. The emergency room was hazy, but she did remember the stitches hurting like hell, the doctor not using enough lidocaine to numb the area. That was probably Conway's doing as well. She remembered leaning against the wall as her picture was taken and stumbling down a long hallway before being dumped unceremoniously in here.

Her head was foggy, the result of two or three too many hits, again courtesy of Conway. She was with it enough to hope it wouldn't be too long before she could use the phone. She didn't have to wait long before a pencil-thin, pimply faced guard with a military buzz cut yelled her name.

"Boarder, time for your phone call," he said, mispronouncing her last name.

Peyton got up, fighting down a wave of nausea and dizziness as she shuffled toward the door. She stopped in front of him and turned around, her hands behind her back. He cuffed her, and she hissed in pain, the abrasions from Conway's restraints raw on her wrists.

They walked down the hall, Peyton squinting through her good eye, trying to keep the harsh overhead lights from driving ice picks farther into her head. They passed through three secured doors before finally entering a small room with a long table bolted to the floor, several stools anchored in front of it. The room smelled like urine and despair.

The guard unlocked her handcuffs. "You've got five minutes."

The man hadn't showered, a distinctive odor emanating from him, and Peyton was grateful she couldn't breathe out of her swollen nose. She picked up the phone and dialed.

"Bernie, it's Peyton. I'm…" She turned to the guard. "Where am I?"

"Fourth Avenue jail."

"I'm in the Fourth Avenue jail. Conway brought me in. I didn't do anything, and I can prove it," she said, putting her hand over the mouthpiece so the guard couldn't hear. Bernie instructed her not to say anything to anyone and said he'd be over within the hour.

Peyton continued to talk as if Bernie was still on the line, drawing out her five minutes of freedom as long as she could.

"Time's up," the guard said and reached over and hung up the phone. If she were actually talking to someone she wouldn't have had any chance to end the call.

She went back to the cell to wait for Bernie. The women didn't hassle her, at least so far, but they would leave, and others would come in. Peyton hoped to be out of here by then.

Fifty minutes later, the same scrawny guard came in and, mispronouncing her name again, informed Peyton her attorney had arrived. Five minutes later, Peyton was seated across from him. Bernard Lerner was in his mid-fifties, with more hair on his face than on his head. He was still tan and trim and didn't lie to her.

"My God, Peyton, what happened?" Bernie asked, standing up when she walked into the room.

Peyton waited until her handcuffs were removed and the guard closed the door behind him, giving them the required attorney-client privacy.

"Conway, my P.O. I didn't do anything, and I can prove it," she said again, mumbling through her fat lip.

"What do you mean? Start at the beginning. Tell me what happened."

Peyton skipped the part about her and Leigh and said, "I have cameras in my apartment. He's come in and been an asshole before."

"What?" Bernie exclaimed.

"Conway has come into my apartment and torn it up," she repeated. "But nothing like last night." Peyton waved at her face, then gave her attorney the full version of Conway's nocturnal visits. "But I knew it would come to this someday. I installed cameras in every room, controlled by an app on my phone. They feed into my laptop. Have Marcus give you a key, and get it before Conway does."

Her attorney sat back in his chair, his pen still poised to take notes, the page on his yellow legal pad blank.

"Jesus, Peyton. This is bad."

"I didn't do anything," she said again, almost pleading. Finally, after way too long, Bernie spoke.

"Conway's petitioned to revoke your probation."

Peyton protested again. "But I didn't do anything."

"He's charged you with not complying with a mandatory drug test and resisting arrest."

"He tossed me a pee cup and demanded I pee in front of him."

"He can't do that." Bernie knew the terms and conditions of her parole.

"I know, and I wasn't going to." Peyton's renewed anger made her head pound again. "As for resisting arrest, that's also bullshit. He handcuffed me and started whaling on me. I never laid a hand on him. It's all on the tape, Bernie. At least I hope to God it is."

"Did anybody witness any of this?" When Peyton hesitated, he said, "Don't lie to me."

"I wasn't alone, but she didn't see him hit me. She was gone by then. She did see him toss the pee cup at me."

Bernie poised his pen on the top line of the paper. "What's her name?"

"I don't want her involved."

"She's already involved, Peyton."

"I don't care."

"Does he know who she is?"

Peyton replayed the conversation Leigh had had on the phone with the 9-1-1 dispatcher. "But I don't want her involved," she said again, adamant that Leigh not be dragged into this.

"What is her name, Peyton? I can subpoena the 9-1-1 records, but I don't think you want me to do that. Then she'll really be involved."

"Her name is Leigh Marshall. She's a member at Copperwind. Marcus can give you her number."

"You don't know it?" Bernie asked.

"It's in my phone in my apartment."

"Okay. I'll get it from him. How is she going to react when I call?"

"I have no idea," Peyton said honestly. "She didn't know."

"That you were on parole?"

"Anything," Peyton said flatly.

"Is she, uh…"

"A one-night stand?" Peyton asked, the question almost sticking in her throat. When Bernie nodded she said, "No. We've been seeing each other for a while."

"Okay. Let me see what I can do. I'll get your laptop and look at the recording. I'll show it to the judge assigned to your case, and if it's as clear as you say, the charges should be dropped and we can keep her out of it. Until then, sit tight." He started to rise from the metal chair.

Panic rose in Peyton's throat, threatening to choke her. Claustrophobia overwhelmed her; her breathing quickened, and her hands started shaking. Bernie sat back down, his beefy hand covering hers. It was little comfort.

"Take a deep breath, Peyton. You're going to be all right. I'll go to your place right now and get the recording in front of the judge as soon as I can. Your arraignment is scheduled for three this afternoon. Hopefully you'll be out of here to have dinner in your own kitchen."

Peyton had pulled herself together by the time her attorney left. The guard escorted her back to her cell, a little rougher than he needed to be, the handcuffs too tight. She'd learned never to complain or it just got worse. When the cell door behind her closed, Peyton sat on the cold, hard metal bench to do the only thing she could—wait.

CHAPTER THIRTY-TWO

S he's what?"

When Leigh had gotten home and collapsed just inside her front door, she remained there until the sun started coming in through the shutters. She'd managed to call her admin and had her cancel her meetings for the day. No way would she be able to function today. She finally managed to get up and into the shower and make it to the restaurant to meet Jill for lunch, after she'd stopped at an AIDS clinic for a blood test. She would make an appointment at her gynecologist this afternoon.

"She's an ex-convict. She killed the man that kidnapped and assaulted her little sister."

Jill dropped her fork, the clatter on her plate causing heads to turn their way. "Holy fuck," Jill said, echoing her own sentiment for hours.

"Was it like self-defense or something?"

"No. From what I read he hadn't gone to trial yet. She just shot him in his driveway."

"Holy mother fuck." Jill fell back in her seat, the shock on her face mirroring how Leigh felt.

"I guess there was a tape or something he made, so it was pretty clear he did it."

"Why did she do it? I mean, I know why she did it, but what did she say?"

"I didn't read where she ever made a statement anywhere."

Jill looked confused. "How did you find out about this?"

"I learned about it at two thirty this morning when her parole officer was standing in her living room."

"What? Wait, what? Are you seeing her? You need to start at the beginning," Jill demanded.

Leigh relayed the events leading up to Peyton's parole officer barging into Peyton's apartment. When she finished, she was exhausted. She'd been up for over thirty-six hours, several of which were sex-filled, the last ten with more than a little emotional shock thrown in.

"Jesus, Leigh. What are you going to do?"

"I certainly can't see her anymore. I can't have that mess in my life. If Larry or anyone else at work found out...I've got enough to deal with. I don't need this spectacle piled on."

"To quote a cliché, she's served her time and paid her dues to society. Doesn't she have the right to start over?"

"Of course she does," Leigh said quickly. "But not as part of my life."

"Leigh, you like this woman. Give her a chance to explain."

"What's to explain? She killed somebody."

"Yeah, but the guy deserves to be dead. Don't you think there are some mitigating circumstances here? I know you're upset—"

"Upset doesn't even begin to describe how I feel," Leigh shot back. "I feel used."

"How did she use you? You just said you two were just having a good time."

"She didn't tell me she'd killed someone, that she'd been in prison," Leigh said, like that was explanation enough.

"Did you tell her that when you were fifteen you broke into your boyfriend's house and stole his T-shirt after he broke up with you?"

"That's not the same."

"No, it's not, but my point is."

"Well, you're going to have to spell it out to me. My mind is mush."

"It's not like you were getting serious and needed to share each other's life stories." Jill stopped, her eyebrows scrunching together.

She looked at Leigh hard, understanding dawning on her face. "You fell for her."

Before Leigh had a chance to refute Jill's observation she said, "Don't lie to yourself, Leigh. I think you're upset because of how it would look having Peyton in your life."

"Don't I have a reason to? She killed somebody, for God's sake. What's my mother going to say? And my dad? Holy crap. He'll shit bricks."

"Aren't you maybe getting ahead of yourself? Have you spoken to her today?"

"No. The last I saw of her she was being tossed into the back of her parole officer's car. I have no idea where she is. Even if I did, she's the one who deceived me. She needs to come to me."

"Will you listen to her?"

"What's there to say, Jill?"

"Oh, for God's sake, Leigh. I know you're brilliant, but there is more to the story here than what you read in a few articles on the Internet."

It was more than a few stories, but Leigh didn't correct her. "It seems pretty cut-and-dried to me."

"How can you be so flippant?"

"I'm not," Leigh snapped, then immediately felt remorse. She had no reason to take it out on Jill, who was only trying to be helpful. "I'm sorry. I've been up since six yesterday morning, and I'm exhausted." She pulled a twenty from her wallet and laid it on top of the bill the waiter had left between them a few minutes ago. "I've got to get some sleep."

Leigh stood and kissed Jill on the cheek. "I'll call you later, okay?" She didn't wait for an answer, just went out the front door to head home.

Leigh was tired, but too tired to sleep. Even though her body was exhausted, her mind was still moving, albeit at a much slower pace.

She didn't want to sit and think. She needed to be busy. She just wanted the entire relationship with Peyton to go away, fade into the background of her brain and not come out again. She knew it was childish to think that if she ignored it, then it hadn't happened. But she just wanted to erase it from her memory.

❖

Peyton wasn't home by dinner but did collapse on her couch in time for the late news. She wasn't the headline, thank God, and was relieved when her name wasn't mentioned anywhere. Somehow, she had managed to escape this ordeal without notice.

Bernie had been able to retrieve her laptop and show the recording to the arraigning judge, who promptly dropped all charges and released her. The director of the parole department had met with her and Bernie for three hours, taking her statement of not only the incident she recorded, but the other times Conway had been in her apartment. He vowed to look into her allegations.

A knock on her door made her jump, but she calmed down when she heard Marcus's voice.

"Peyton? You okay?"

Peyton's arms were heavy with fatigue as she opened the door.

"Hey," Marcus said, looking at her.

Peyton knew she must look a mess. She was wearing the same clothes she'd had on yesterday, complete with jailhouse funk. She'd seen dark smudges under her eyes when she used the bathroom just before Bernie picked her up.

"Hey" was just about all she could say.

"You okay?" Marcus asked again, concern in his voice. He didn't make any move to come in, and Peyton was grateful for that. She wasn't up to twenty questions or entertaining.

"Yeah."

"Need anything?"

"No. Just to get some sleep." She probably wouldn't, though, the nightmare of almost returning to Nelson too fresh in her mind.

"Come over for coffee in the morning if you feel up to it." That was Marcus's way of giving her the option to talk if she wanted to.

Bernie had told Peyton that Marcus had come to the jail, but since he wasn't allowed to see her, Bernie had managed to convince him to go home. He looked almost as tired as she felt.

"Thanks. I might take you up on that."

Marcus turned and walked back down the stairs, and Peyton closed and locked the door. Bernie had returned her laptop, and as tired as she was, Peyton made sure it was ready to record again, if need be. She refused to be caught off guard if Conway came back, this time looking for revenge.

It was after midnight when her head hit the pillow. It was the pillow where Leigh had lain her head, and she inhaled deeply. Leigh's scent still clung to the fabric, and a thousand images flashed in her mind. Leigh straddling her, her back arched, head thrown back in pleasure. Peyton's hands covering her breasts as Leigh rocked against her. Leigh looking at her, her mouth between Peyton's legs. Leigh laughing when Peyton tickled her, sighing in pleasure, calling out Peyton's name every time she came.

She replayed every time she and Leigh were intimate, knowing memories would be all she'd have from this point forward. Peyton rolled onto her side. Sleep refused to come so she got up and dressed, grabbed her keys, and headed out the door.

CHAPTER THIRTY-THREE

L eigh jumped at the knock on her front door. It was late, and it was either Peyton or maybe even that sleazy guy—her parole officer. He frightened her, and she didn't want to see Peyton until she had a better handle on her emotions and a grip on the new reality of who she was.

Leigh had fallen for Peyton, hard. She was strikingly attractive and had a body that made her senseless. In a very short time, Peyton had learned how to make her beg for release and plead for more at the same time, and she wanted to spend the rest of her life discovering every nuance of her. Until her recent discovery.

Leigh didn't know if she was angry that Peyton hadn't trusted her enough to tell her or scared shitless because of what she'd done and what it implied. Logic and emotions were at war inside her, and she was exhausted with the up-and-down and back-and-forth attempt to make sense of it all. She needed peace and quiet to sort it out, and being in the same room with Peyton would definitely not bring that.

Peyton made her crazy. She turned her orderly world catawampus, which made her very uncomfortable. She avoided chaos at all costs, studying everything at varying angles and weighing the pros and cons. She'd been determined to be viewed as a professional and not labeled a typical woman, with all the stereotypical emotions and weaknesses that accompanied that title, however much bullshit it was. She'd practiced long and hard and trained herself to process a magnitude of information in an instant and make well-reason decisions.

Since Peyton had come into her life, she couldn't think straight, often daydreamed, and felt like a schoolgirl with her first crush. She was full of energy, almost euphoric, and butterflies flitted around in her stomach all day. She was a mess and, after the last twenty hours, a fucking mess.

"Leigh?"

A mass of emotions churned as Leigh thought about pretending she wasn't home. She was relieved it was Peyton but wasn't ready to see her.

"Leigh, please open the door." Peyton's voice was muffled by the thick, metal door.

Leigh opened the door but only a few inches. She needed the barrier between them to keep her head straight. The instant she saw Peyton standing in the warm glow of her porch light, she knew that wouldn't work.

"What do you want, Peyton? It's late." Leigh offered the time as an excuse, hoping that would make her just go away. She didn't know if she had the strength to do it herself.

"I need to talk to you."

"Peyton, I'm exhausted. I ca...don't want to talk to you right now."

"Leigh. Let me explain."

"You should have told me before you fucked me!" Leigh exploded, her nerves closer to the surface than she realized. She was shocked at her words and the emotions behind them.

Peyton stepped back as if she'd slapped her, hurt and anger clear on her face. She pulled her lips in and frowned. "If that's the way you think about what we shared, I can't do anything to change your mind. But you owe me the courtesy of listening to my side of the story."

"I owe you?" Leigh asked dumbfounded. "*I* owe *you*?" she repeated. "I'm not the one who kept something as big as this to herself. I owe you?" she asked again, at a loss at this entire conversation.

"Leigh, it had nothing to do with us—"

"Nothing to do with us? Are you out of your fucking mind? It has everything to do with us. You killed someone. And you can actually stand there and tell me it has nothing to do with us?" Leigh had fully opened the door some time during the last few seconds.

"If you'd have let me finish, you would have heard me say that it had nothing to do with us in the beginning. I thought we were just…a…a thing that would burn itself out. I didn't see any need for you to know."

"Don't you tell any of the women you sleep with?"

"It's not like an STD," Peyton said, running her hands through her hair. "They're not going to catch something. If you'd just let me—"

"And what are you going to say? Whatever I want to hear so we can continue this, this…" Leigh waved her hands between them. "What did you call it…thing?"

Peyton stood straighter, her expression serious. "I never lied to you."

"And lying by omission is okay?"

Peyton put her hands up as if signaling her surrender. "Look. We're not going to get anywhere standing in your doorway. May I come in?"

"No."

"Leigh, please."

Leigh felt her resolve waver, and before it did, she said, "I can't talk to you right now, Peyton." She closed the door before the memories of how she felt when in Peyton's arms changed her mind.

CHAPTER THIRTY-FOUR

Y ou had cameras on us?" Leigh asked, sounding both appalled and furious.

"No," Peyton said quickly, trying to defuse the situation. "I only used them when Conway came in, and you saw why."

They were sitting in a back booth in the Copperwind restaurant. It was six days after she knocked on Leigh's front door, and Peyton had been shocked when Leigh called and agreed to see her.

"I turned them on just before I opened the door."

That explanation seemed to appease Leigh, though she might not be happy when she realized the one in the bedroom had probably caught her getting dressed.

"Conway is a prick, and I knew he was doing stuff he had no authority or right to do."

"Like that?" Leigh asked, motioning to Peyton's bruised face and the black stitches on her cheek.

"He never laid a hand on me before. It was always words and innuendos and sarcasm. He—"

Leigh held her hands up. "Wait. Start at the beginning. The very beginning."

"I killed someone," Peyton said simply, because it was that simple. Sure, there were circumstances, there always were. But the details didn't matter.

Peyton told her story. It was factual and without emotion. She'd long ago buried those emotions; she'd had to in order to survive.

Slowly and methodically Peyton recounted the events of the days leading up to the morning she went to prison.

Many different emotions crossed Leigh's face. Shock, horror, disgust, fear, anger, pain, and many more. Somewhere in there, Peyton thought she caught a glimpse of compassion.

"And you couldn't have told me before we…" Leigh gasped and put her hand to her mouth as if she wanted to throw up.

Peyton didn't answer. She had nothing left to say.

"I'm sorry. I can't have this in my life." Leigh slid out of the booth.

Peyton didn't watch her walk away.

❖

"She killed someone." The words kept echoing in Leigh's head like the dull throb of a bad headache. The shutters were closed in her living room, the lights dim. Jill was seated beside her on the couch.

"She told her story in almost clinical terms and added very little emotion to the facts. It was almost as if she were reading the investigation report written by the detectives." It had taken two beers for Leigh to tell Jill all the events leading up to this point. "I'm not even an armchair psychologist, but is that her way of distancing herself from the actual event? I don't know if I'd be so unemotional. But then again, it happened more than ten years ago. Do you ever put something like that away and move on?" Those were only a few of the questions Leigh had been asking herself. She was rambling, her thoughts still scattered.

"It seems as though she's trying to," Jill said quietly.

"What am I supposed to do?" Leigh asked, now pacing the room. "Does she expect me to simply say, 'Hey, no problem. People kill each other every day. It doesn't reflect on their character or whether they could or would do it again.' What dream is she living in? And what do I say to my friends and my family? 'Mom, Dad, this is Peyton. She's an ex-con out on parole for murder. She can't leave town, so going to the lake house this summer is out of the question.' That would bring all conversation to a halt around the bar-b-que pit."

"And what about at a dinner party or a company function where spouses are expected to attend? Where small talk is abundant, questions asked, and stories told? Everybody will know. That kind of juicy gossip spreads like wildfire. What will my coworkers think of her? And Larry? He'll drop a gasket. Will they even give her a chance? And, my God, what will they think of me? That we were prison pen pals? Jesus, I sound like a made-for-TV trashy movie. It makes my stomach turn."

"Why don't you sit down? Watching you go back and forth like a Ping-Pong ball over a net is making me dizzy."

"And what will I think after a few years?" Leigh kept pacing. "What will our life be like in five years? Ten? Would I resent the limitations or microscope on our lives? Would I always worry that it would happen again? Would Peyton lose control and hurt me? Could she?" She didn't expect Jill to answer.

"And what about the family of the man she killed? What if they find out where we live? Would they cause trouble for Peyton and, by association, me? Would we be on the news, the media camping out on our doorstep? My office?" Leigh stopped and looked at Jill. "My God, Jill. I watched some old news footage, and it was a feeding frenzy. The sharks were after her."

"Leigh, you yourself said it was over ten years ago. The public loses interest after three days."

Leigh looked at Jill. "This isn't something you prepare yourself for. How many other people are in my shoes? Is there a Facebook page for girlfriends of women who killed someone who deserved to be killed? It wouldn't surprise me if there were. Weirder shit is out there. And what are we going to tell our kids? Will they suffer because of what their mom did twenty or thirty years ago? Would they be denied government clearance for the job they always dreamed of? Disqualified from college? Will this be the proverbial sins of the fathers?"

"Leigh, for God's sake, sit down," Jill said harshly, grabbing her by the arm and pulling her onto the couch next to her. "When was the last time you ate something?"

"I'm not hungry."

"When was the last time you ate something?" Jill asked a little more forcefully.

"Lunch, yesterday," Leigh admitted.

"Yesterday? Jesus, Leigh. No wonder you're off your rocker. You need some food. It's after seven. That's over thirty hours ago. Your body needs fuel even if your stomach says otherwise."

Jill fixed them both a grilled ham-and-cheese sandwich, and Leigh picked at hers, finishing half. A full glass of milk sat on the table in front of her. Jill dried the frying pan and wiped her hands on a dish towel before sitting beside her.

"Feel better?"

"Yes."

"At the risk of winding you up again, it sounds like you're in love with Peyton."

"What?" Leigh asked, the clenching in her gut growing tighter.

"Before you start denying it, let me explain," Jill said, putting her hands up in front of her as if stopping an avalanche of words. "Did you hear what you said?" Leigh remained silent. "Things like introducing Peyton to your family and coworkers. What it was going to be like five or ten years from now? What do we tell our kids?" Jill gazed at her, her face soft and understanding. "Leigh, honey," Jill said gently, laying her hand on Leigh's forearm. "You are in love with this woman."

"No, I'm not," Leigh said, a little too forcefully.

"Yes, you are."

"No." Realization crept into her brain. "I can't be."

"Why? Because of her past? We all have one, Leigh. When we fall in love, we either accept it and deal with it or move on. It doesn't sound like you want to move on."

Jill's words thundered in her brain like a fast-moving freight train. In love with Peyton? In love with Peyton? She'd been in love once or twice, and both times felt nothing like this. When she'd walked away from those women, it had hurt, but she hadn't experienced the gut-wrenching, soul-ripping void of loneliness and despair that filled her now.

Was she truly in love with Peyton? Did she want to see Peyton's face across the pillow from her every night? Lose all control when she touched her? Taste her hot, delicious kisses? Did she want to be the only woman in Peyton's life? The one she hurried home to and dragged herself away from? Why did it feel like someone had reached inside her chest and yanked out her insides? Did she want to live the rest of her life without her, no matter the consequences?

Chapter Thirty-five

Peyton's knees buckled from the pain. She knew it was Conway. It couldn't be anyone else. It had been almost three weeks since he barged into her apartment and threw her life to shit. She'd just finished her testimony detailing his actions in her apartment to the civil-service board. Public policy in the state allowed an employee on the verge of termination to receive a hearing in front of a panel consisting of two civilians and three city employees. In this case, the panel was all men, and if Peyton hadn't had the video, she doubted Conway would lose his job. She'd stopped for a quick sandwich and was walking back to her truck when she was grabbed from behind and hit in her right kidney. She'd suffered a similar hit in Nelson, and she'd had blood in her pee for a week.

"Get up, bitch," Conway snarled in her ear. He dragged her to her feet by a handful of her shirt and slammed her face-first against the hood of her truck, her nose crunching like he'd broken it. She fought the blackness that threatened to overtake her. No way could she pass out now. She'd be lucky if she woke up alive if she did. He wrenched one arm behind her back so far she thought it would break.

"This is all your fault," he hissed, spittle blanketing her good ear. "Because of you I'm going to lose my job and my pension." He emphasized the last word by shifting her arm a little higher up her back. "You and your sweet little deal and that sweet little piece of ass." His breath reeked of whiskey, and his words were slightly slurred.

Peyton's blood raced faster at Conway's reference to Leigh.

"Maybe when I'm done with you, I'll pay her a visit." He had Peyton pinned against her truck and ground his pelvis into her. He didn't need to be any more explicit, his intention clear.

Peyton struggled to catch her breath and clear her head. She was in a public parking lot, but unfortunately not a highly trafficked one at this particular moment. Stars danced behind her eyes, but they grew fewer with every fill of her lungs. She had to get out of this situation and get out of it fast.

"What do you want?" she managed to choke out, her breath still ragged, blood spattering on the hood in front of her.

"What do I want? What do I want?" Conway said, then said it again. The longer he talked, the more she was able to get oxygen to her brain. Keep him talking long enough, and someone was bound to see them.

"What I want," he sneered, "is for you to go back into that room and say you made it all up, but that's not going to happen because of your fucking amateur video."

When he said it that way, her future sounded bleak. She managed to turn her head to the side, and blood poured out of her nose.

"I want my pound of flesh before I have to leave town. If I can't throw your ass back in Nelson, then you'll suffer another way."

"This is not going to help your case."

"I don't have a case." He was mocking her. "I was good at my job, one of the best. I did shit and took ex-cons nobody wanted. And after twenty-five years, this is what I get? Nothing. All because a privileged killer was released early."

"You let me go, and I won't say anything about this."

Conway laughed, his disgusting breath hot on her neck.

"Do you think I'm that stupid?" He leaned his excessive body weight into her. "I asked you a question, bitch. Answer me," he growled.

Conway was proving that he was an idiot, but Peyton kept her opinion to herself. "What are you going to do?" Probably not the best question, Peyton thought, but she wasn't going to just do nothing and take his shit. Not again. Not ever.

"What are you going to do, Conway? Beat me up? Again? A lot of good it did you the last time." Peyton knew she was antagonizing him, pushing him further out of control. A man like Conway would lose it and make a mistake. When he did, she'd be ready.

Conway yanked her up and shoved her toward the passenger door of her truck. "Shut up and get in," he said quickly.

Peyton knew if she got into the truck with him, her chances of surviving would diminish substantially. "No."

Conway's fist connected in the same spot as his first blow had, and she staggered again, the pain so severe she vomited up her lunch.

"God damn it, I said get in." With his free hand he reached inside her front pocket and pulled out her keys. He unlocked the door and shoved her inside. "Move over," he said, pushing her behind the wheel. He put the key in the ignition and started the truck. "Drive," he commanded.

Through her haze of pain and the swelling of her eyes and nose, Peyton saw Conway had a gun in his hand, pointed at her. Her odds plummeted. Peyton put the truck in gear and pulled out of the parking lot.

"Where are we going?" Peyton asked, trying to focus on the road in front of her. The white lines were blurred, and the lane seemed much too small for the truck to remain in the middle.

"Just shut up and drive." Conway wiped sweat from his forehead, his breathing labored.

Peyton knew that no way was she going to drive herself to some secluded place where Conway could kill her and dump her body. The more in focus her surroundings became, the more she saw that people were staring at her as she drove down the street. The bleeding from her nose had eased to a trickle, but the front of her shirt was covered with blood. She knew bruises were starting to form under her eyes that, along with her nose, had started to swell.

Conway reached into his back pocket and pulled out a flask. With his attention on unscrewing the lid, Peyton risked a look at the woman in the car beside her. She held up her cell phone, indicating if Peyton wanted her to call 9-1-1. Peyton nodded once.

The light turned green, and a block later Peyton saw the woman in the car pull in behind her, talking excitedly on the phone. The woman gave her a thumbs-up, and Peyton gave a silent thank you.

Traffic was light, and, in between ranting and raving about what she'd done to him, Conway directed her onto the interstate. Peyton kept glancing in the rearview mirror looking for the police, her fuzzy brain scrambling for a plan. If the police stopped them, there was a good chance Conway would simply shoot her. At this close range and given the caliber of his gun, she'd be dead before the ambulance arrived. She hadn't gone more than a mile or two before she saw a car speeding up behind her. It didn't have lights or any markings, and she suspected it was an unmarked patrol car. Just as it was about to overtake them, a plan formed in her mind.

With her right foot still on the accelerator, she lightly tapped the brake with her left, but not hard enough to be detected. She repeated the action several times, hoping the driver behind her understood. Bracing herself, Peyton slammed on the brake with both feet.

The truck skidded on the pavement, fishtailing several times before coming to a stop. Peyton opened the door, jumped out of the truck, and ran, seeking cover behind the tailgate. The car behind her slid to a stop, missing her back bumper by less than a foot. The driver's door flew open, and a uniformed officer got out, his gun drawn.

"Hands on your head," he shouted from behind the cover of his door.

Peyton quickly complied and dropped to her knees. Her head was swimming and she almost passed out, but somehow she managed to do exactly what the officer told her to.

"Passenger," the officer said, his voice broadcasting over the loudspeaker. "Put your hands where I can see them."

He repeated the command two more times before a marked patrol car slid to a stop behind them both.

In a matter of minutes, the officers had Peyton in the back of the patrol car and Conway on his stomach on the side of the road, his hands cuffed behind his back, blood coming from a gash on his forehead. He hadn't had his seat belt on, and when she stomped on the brakes, he hit the windshield. It took the better part of an hour before they sorted everything out and Marcus was allowed to come take Peyton home.

A trip to the emergency room, an icepack, and three prescriptions later, Peyton fell into bed.

CHAPTER THIRTY-SIX

Two weeks later, the bruising and swelling had subsided enough for Peyton to return to work. She'd actually gone back three days after Conway assaulted her in the parking lot but stayed out of sight of the guests and members. The tape on her nose was gone, and the bruises under her eyes had turned from colorful shades of purple and green to slight smudges of yellow.

"Leigh cancelled her lessons," Marcus said, turning the pages in the appointment book. "She didn't reschedule."

"She probably won't," Peyton said before she realized that her comment would elicit questions from her brother.

"Is there something you're not telling me, Peyton?" Marcus asked, his eagle eyes never missing anything.

Peyton fidgeted. What she and Leigh had done involved much more than socializing. She didn't want to put her brother in an awkward position, one she herself was ashamed to be in. She should have had better control when it came to Leigh. She knew better and understood the problems her actions could cause Marcus. She should have kept her distance, but the chemistry between them was explosive, and she'd been without that spark for far too long. Regrettably, she had a burning need to touch that flame again.

But all that didn't matter. Leigh was out of her life, and Peyton saw no need to bring it all up. "No. I'm just still a little tired, I guess."

Marcus looked at Peyton so hard she was afraid he could read her mind. Finally, he asked, "Are you good to make a cart run?"

"Yeah. I'm fine," Peyton lied. Maybe a little fresh air and sunshine would do her good.

"Leigh must feel her game has improved. She's out there now with some guy named," Marcus flipped the page back in his reservation book, "Larry Taylor."

❖

"Nice drive." Larry complimented the way Leigh's ball sailed into the air and landed perfectly in the middle of the fourth fairway. Their scheduled game had been changed twice, and they'd finally teed off an hour ago on a bright, sunny Saturday morning.

"Thanks," Leigh said, absentminded. She hadn't slept much the past few nights in anticipation of today, and it wasn't because she was playing a round of golf with her boss. They would be at Copperwind, and Peyton would be here. She worked every Saturday, and Leigh had been looking for her the entire morning. She wasn't sure if she wanted to see her.

Her game today was respectable, but clearly Larry was a much better golfer than she was. Leigh remembered everything Peyton had taught her without overanalyzing it, and her game was solid. Very much unlike her game with Stark and her life since meeting Peyton.

"So, tell me, Leigh. How are you settling in?" Larry asked, referring to her new job.

"Good," she fibbed. "It's pretty much what I expected, but I think I've adjusted quickly." Fib number two. "How do you think things are going?"

"You're doing great. I've asked around over the past few weeks, and they all said the same."

"Would they say any different?" Leigh wondered out loud.

"Why do you ask?"

Leigh looked over Larry's shoulder and saw Peyton's cart approach. Her body instinctively remembered how it felt to be held in her strong arms, caressed by her gentle hands, driven to ecstasy by her skillful mouth. She flushed all over, and her heart rate picked up.

She had less than a minute to decide. She'd thought about it for weeks and hadn't yet reached any conclusion until this very moment.

"Good morning," Peyton said, only glancing at Leigh. "Can I get you two something to drink?"

Leigh's heart skipped at the warm timbre of Peyton's voice. She remembered another time when it had whispered in her ear, "Come for me." But her attention was immediately drawn to the remnants of bruising on Peyton's face. Her sunglasses hid most of them, but Leigh knew every inch of Peyton's face, and there was no hiding it from her. Somehow, she managed to ask for a bottle of water, when she really wanted a shot or two of Canadian Club.

Peyton was counting change from Larry's twenty-dollar bill he'd handed her for their two waters when she said, "I need to tell you something, Larry. Peter Stark is a problem."

"I beg your pardon?" Larry said, after almost choking on his swallow of water. Peyton stopped counting his change and stared at her.

"Peter is a problem," she repeated, more confident now that she'd gotten the first words out of her mouth. "He's homophobic, probably a racist, and he's definitely an ass."

"I think you'd better explain," her boss said seriously. He took his change from Peyton and thanked her.

"When he and I golfed in that tournament benefitting the foster kids, he made some very inappropriate, disparaging, insulting comments about a woman." Leigh proceeded to tell Larry, almost word for word, what Stark had said to, and about, Peyton. Larry was pale when she finished.

"I should have said something right then, but I admit I was a bit intimidated by him and was so shocked to hear that kind of talk come out of his mouth, I didn't do anything. That's the biggest mistake I've ever made in my life. I will never again not speak up when something is wrong, no matter who it concerns, and I'm doing so now."

Larry stared at Leigh, and it was a long moment before he said anything. Peyton was still standing across from them.

"Do you have anyone to corroborate this accusation?"

Leigh looked at Peyton, who was eyeing her seriously. She gave her a nod so imperceptive Leigh almost missed it. Her resolve was solid.

She turned back to Larry, looking him straight in the eye. "Yes, I do." She hesitated another second before plunging on. "If he thinks that way about lesbians, then he thinks that way about me, and I refuse to be spoken about like that again."

Leigh wasn't in the closet at work, but she also never openly spoke about her private life. First, because there was nothing to tell, and second, because it wasn't anyone's business. This was a game changer for her.

Larry studied her as if judging her authenticity. Finally, he said, "I believe you. I may need the names."

Leigh was overcome with waves of relief. She honestly didn't know if he would believe her or take the side of his long-time employee. Her respect for him skyrocketed.

"I'll have them on your desk first thing Monday morning."

"Peyton, can I talk to you for a minute?" Leigh wasn't sure if Peyton would stop or simply keep walking into the clubhouse. When she turned to look at her, Leigh was suddenly more than a little nervous.

"I'll get you the names," Peyton said, her voice flat.

"What?"

"The names. Of the others in your group who heard what Stark said."

It took a moment for Leigh to attach Peyton's comment to a question. She finally got it. "That's not what I want to talk to you about." Before she could say anything, Peyton removed her sunglasses, her look hard.

"My God, Peyton. Are you okay?" Leigh asked. She started to touch the discolored skin but stopped herself. "What happened?"

"Conway. But it doesn't concern you." Peyton's voice was cold and emotionless.

Leigh didn't know what to say. She'd made it clear that it wasn't any of her business, as Peyton had so accurately said. She'd lost track of what she wanted to talk to Peyton about. Peyton waited, impatience written on her face and in her body language.

"I'm sorry," Leigh said. "I'm sorry for everything. For the way Stark spoke to you, the way I didn't stand up and tell him to shut the fuck up. The way I reacted when I…when you…"

"Don't apologize, Leigh. I don't want or need you to." Peyton's voice was harsh. "I also don't need your pity. I'm a big girl, an even bigger one because of what I did. I took responsibility for my actions, paid the price, and am moving on with my life." Peyton hesitated, her eyes dark with uncertainty, pinning Leigh with their intensity. "With or without you."

Leigh was stunned. When did this happen? When had a romp of casual, no-strings-attached sex become a lifeline she didn't want to lose?

Chapter Thirty-seven

"You're in love."

"Excuse me?" Peyton asked after wiping her chin from the after-dinner coffee that spewed out of her mouth.

"You heard me," Olivia said. "Who is she?"

Peyton was taken aback by Olivia's statement, which wasn't a question. They were sitting on the back patio, the coffee in her cup still steaming. It had been three days since she'd seen Leigh.

"Don't try to pretend you don't know what I'm talking about."

"Her name is Leigh Marshall." It felt good to say Leigh's name out loud.

"What's the problem? No woman in love looks like you do right now."

Peyton didn't know where to start. She'd barely been able to get out of bed the past several mornings, and she felt like someone had ripped out her guts and tossed them into a bucket.

"Tell me about her. She must be pretty special to have captured your heart," Olivia said, her voice gentle and inviting. She sat back in her chair, settling in for a long conversation.

"She's warm and kind, and she makes me laugh and think. She makes me want to be a better person, to do my best in everything I do." Peyton went on to tell Olivia everything about Leigh, finishing with, "She cares deeply for other people."

"Like ex-cons on parole?"

"She doesn't want anything to do with me," Peyton said, defeated.

"How so? You've served your time." Olivia said like it was just that simple.

"She has a pretty big, important job. She's probably afraid of how her company would react if they found out about me. God only knows about her family. And the whole Conway scene. It was ugly, and she didn't need to see that."

"I get it." Olivia pursed her lips and frowned. "So?"

"So?" Peyton asked, a little angry. "What am I supposed to do? I can't change history." Peyton told Olivia the ultimatum she'd left Leigh with.

Olivia was looking at her so intently she started to squirm.

"Do you love her?"

Peyton had thought about that question for days. The way she felt, the pain in her chest, the sleepless nights. The paralyzing fear that Leigh wouldn't be in her life. She had no other answer to Olivia's question. "Yes. But she wants nothing to do with me."

"Leigh," Peyton said, after yanking open her front door. She'd tried to ignore the knocking, but whoever it was, was insistent. It was obvious they weren't going away. She didn't want to see anybody and was in no mood to entertain guests. Leigh was the last person she expected to see standing on her doorstep the next evening.

"Hi," Leigh said tentatively, her eyes darting back and forth between Peyton's and the ground. "I hope I'm not interrupting anything."

Peyton snapped herself from the shock of seeing Leigh again. "No, uhh, would you like to come in?" She opened the door for Leigh to enter.

"Could we sit outside? Under the tree." Leigh pointed to a large tree in Marcus and Olivia's backyard.

The tree was mature, its canopy at least thirty feet wide. She and Marcus had built a bench circling the base and added soft lights for nights just like this. It was her favorite spot when she needed to think.

"Sure. Would you like something to drink?" Peyton asked, surprised she remembered her manners.

Leigh shook her head. "No, thanks."

Peyton closed the door behind her and followed Leigh across the neatly manicured yard to the tree. She used her hand and wiped leaves that had fallen in the last day or two off the bench.

"It's beautiful out here," Leigh said, gazing into the sky on the horizon. Peyton was looking at Leigh.

"Yes, it is."

"Are those crickets?"

Peyton wasn't in the mood to make small talk. She didn't want to dance around why Leigh was here, so she asked. It was several moments before Leigh answered, her eyes still on the night sky.

"I don't know. I can't seem to get you out of my head."

"But you don't want me beside you."

Leigh turned to look at Peyton. "I do, but—"

"There is no but, Leigh. I either am or I'm not."

"It's not that simple."

"Isn't it?" Peyton asked, turning to fully face her. Leigh was breathtaking, heartbreakingly beautiful. "I love you, and you either love me enough to spend the rest of your life with me and whatever that brings—the good, the bad and the ugly—or you don't."

"I'm afraid."

"So am I," Peyton said, her voice softening. "I can't breathe when I'm around you. I can't think. I took a chance being with you because I couldn't imagine my life without you. I don't want to miss this chance at happiness. I don't want to walk away from you." Peyton took a deep breath. "But if you can't accept me, all of me, then I will. Because I won't settle for less."

When Leigh didn't say anything, Peyton rose. Her heart was breaking, but her legs were steady. She had no idea what she was going to do now, but her resolve was firm. She walked the dozen dark, shadowy yards to her door.

"Peyton!"

Peyton spun around, catching Leigh when she leaped into her arms. Leigh wrapped her hand around the back of Peyton's head and drew her down into a hot, passionate, possessive kiss. The sleek slide of Leigh's tongue and the pounding of her heart pushed away any thoughts of ever letting this wonderful woman out of her life. And in that moment, Peyton felt as though she had truly been paroled.

The End

About the Author

Julie Cannon divides her time by being a corporate suit, a wife, mom, sister, friend, and writer. Julie and her wife have lived in at least a half a dozen states, traveled around the world, and have an unending supply of dedicated friends. And of course, the most important people in their lives are their three kids: #1, Dude, and the Devine Miss Em.

With the release of *Fore Play*, Julie will have seventeen books published by Bold Strokes Books. Her first novel, *Come and Get Me*, was a finalist for the Golden Crown Literary Society's Best Lesbian Romance and Debut Author Awards. In 2012, her ninth novel, *Rescue Me*, was a finalist as Best Lesbian Romance from the prestigious Lambda Literary Society, and *I Remember* won the Golden Crown Literary Society's Best Lesbian Romance in 2014. Julie has also published five short stories in Bold Strokes anthologies. www.JulieCannon.com

Books Available from Bold Strokes Books

Breakthrough by Kris Bryant. Falling for a sexy ranger is one thing, but is the possibility of love worth giving up the career Kennedy Wells has always dreamed of? (978-1-63555-179-2)

Certain Requirements by Elinor Zimmerman. Phoenix has always kept her love of kinky submission strictly behind the bedroom door and inside the bounds of romantic relationships, until she meets Kris Andersen. (978-1-63555-195-2)

Dark Euphoria by Ronica Black. When a high-profile case drops in Detective Maria Diaz's lap, she forges ahead only to discover this case, and her main suspect, aren't like any other. (978-1-63555-141-9)

Fore Play by Julie Cannon. Executive Leigh Marshall falls hard for Peyton Broader, her golf pro...and an ex-con. Will she risk sabotaging her career for love? (978-1-63555-102-0)

Love Came Calling by CA Popovich. Can a romantic looking for a long-term, committed relationship and a jaded cynic too busy for love conquer life's struggles and find their way to what matters most? (978-1-63555-205-8)

Outside the Law by Carsen Taite. Former sweethearts Tanner Cohen and Sydney Braswell must work together on a federal task force to see justice served, but will they choose to embrace their second chance at love? (978-1-63555-039-9)

The Princess Deception by Nell Stark. When journalist Missy Duke realizes Prince Sebastian is really his twin sister Viola in disguise, she plays along, but when sparks flare between them, will the double deception doom their fairy-tale romance? (978-1-62639-979-2)

The Smell of Rain by Cameron MacElvee. Reyha Arslan, a wise and elegant woman with a tragic past, shows Chrys that there's still beauty to embrace and reason to hope despite the world's cruelty. (978-1-63555-166-2)

The Talebearer by Sheri Lewis Wohl. Liz's visions show her the faces of the lost and the killers who took their lives. As one by one, the murdered are found, a stranger works to stop Liz before the serial killer is brought to justice. (978-1-63555-126-6)

White Wings Weeping by Lesley Davis. The world is full of discord and hatred, but how much of it is just human nature when an evil with sinister intent is invading people's hearts? (978-1-63555-191-4)

A Call Away by KC Richardson. Can a businesswoman from a big city find the answers she's looking for, and possibly love, on a small-town farm? (978-1-63555-025-2)

Berlin Hungers by Justine Saracen. Can the love between an RAF woman and the wife of a Luftwaffe pilot, former enemies, survive in besieged Berlin during the aftermath of World War II? (978-1-63555-116-7)

Blend by Georgia Beers. Lindsay and Piper are like night and day. Working together won't be easy, but not falling in love might prove the hardest job of all. (978-1-63555-189-1)

Hunger for You by Jenny Frame. Principe of an ancient vampire clan Byron Debrek must save her one true love from falling into the hands of her enemies and into the middle of a vampire war. (978-1-63555-168-6)

Mercy by Michelle Larkin. FBI Special Agent Mercy Parker and psychic ex-profiler Piper Vasey learn to love again as they race to stop a man with supernatural gifts who's bent on annihilating humankind. (978-1-63555-202-7)

Pride and Porters by Charlotte Greene. Will pride and prejudice prevent these modern-day lovers from living happily ever after? (978-1-63555-158-7)

Rocks and Stars by Sam Ledel. Kyle's struggle to own who she is and what she really wants may end up landing her on the bench and without the woman of her dreams. (978-1-63555-156-3)

The Boss of Her: Office Romance Novellas by Julie Cannon, Aurora Rey, and M. Ullrich. Going to work never felt so good. Three office romance novellas from talented writers Julie Cannon, Aurora Rey, and M. Ullrich. (978-1-63555-145-7)

The Deep End by Ellie Hart. When family ties become entangled in murder and deception, it's time to find a way out... (978-1-63555-288-1)

A Country Girl's Heart by Dena Blake. When Kat Jackson gets a second chance at love, following her heart will prove the hardest decision of all. (978-1-63555-134-1)

Dangerous Waters by Radclyffe. Life, death, and war on the home front. Two women join forces against a powerful opponent, nature itself. (978-1-63555-233-1)

Fury's Death by Brey Willows. When all we hold sacred fails, who will be there to save us? (978-1-63555-063-4)

It's Not a Date by Heather Blackmore. Kade's desire to keep things with Jen on a professional level is in Jen's best interest. Yet what's in Kade's best interest...is Jen. (978-1-63555-149-5)

Killer Winter by Kay Bigelow. Just when she thought things could get no worse, homicide Lieutenant Leah Samuels learns the woman she loves has betrayed her in devastating ways. (978-1-63555-177-8)

Score by MJ Williamz. Will an addiction to pain pills destroy Ronda's chance with the woman she loves or will she come out on top and score a happily ever after? (978-1-62639-807-8)

Spring's Wake by Aurora Rey. When wanderer Willa Lange falls for Provincetown B&B owner Nora Calhoun, will past hurts and a fifteen-year age gap keep them from finding love? (978-1-63555-035-1)

The Northwoods by Jane Hoppen. When Evelyn Bauer, disguised as her dead husband, George, travels to a Northwoods logging camp to work, she and the camp cook Sarah Bell forge a friendship fraught with both tenderness and turmoil. (978-1-63555-143-3)

Truth or Dare by C. Spencer. For a group of six lesbian friends, life changes course after one long snow-filled weekend. (978-1-63555-148-8)

A Heart to Call Home by Jeannie Levig. When Jessie Weldon returns to her hometown after thirty years, can she and her childhood crush Dakota Scott heal the tragic past that links them? (978-1-63555-059-7)

Children of the Healer by Barbara Ann Wright. Life becomes desperate for ex-soldier Cordelia Ross when the indigenous aliens of her planet are drawn into a civil war and old enemies linger in the shadows. Book Three of the Godfall Series. (978-1-63555-031-3)

Hearts Like Hers by Melissa Brayden. Coffee shop owner Autumn Primm is ready to cut loose and live a little, but is the baggage that comes with out-of-towner Kate Carpenter too heavy for anything long term? (978-1-63555-014-6)

Love at Cooper's Creek by Missouri Vaun. Shaw Daily flees corporate life to find solace in the rural Blue Ridge Mountains, but escapism eludes her when her attentions are captured by small town beauty Kate Elkins. (978-1-62639-960-0)

Somewhere Over Lorain Road by Bud Gundy. Over forty years after murder allegations shattered the Esker family, can Don Esker find the true killer and clear his dying father's name? (978-1-63555-124-2)

Twice in a Lifetime by PJ Trebelhorn. Detective Callie Burke can't deny the growing attraction to her late friend's widow, Taylor Fletcher, who also happens to own the bar where Callie's sister works. (978-1-63555-033-7)

Undiscovered Affinity by Jane Hardee. Will a no strings attached affair be enough to break Olivia's control and convince Cardic that love does exist? (978-1-63555-061-0)

Between Sand and Stardust by Tina Michele. Are the lifelong bonds of love strong enough to conquer time, distance, and heartache when Haven Thorne and Willa Bennette are given another chance at forever? (978-1-62639-940-2)

Charming the Vicar by Jenny Frame. When magician and atheist Finn Kane seeks refuge in an English village after a spiritual crisis, can local vicar Bridget Claremont restore her faith in life and love? (978-1-63555-029-0)

Data Capture by Jesse J. Thoma. Lola Walker is undercover on the hunt for cybercriminals while trying not to notice the woman who might be perfectly wrong for her for all the right reasons. (978-1-62639-985-3)

Epicurean Delights by Renee Roman. Ariana Marks had no idea a leisure swim would lead to being rescued, in more ways than one, by the charismatic Hudson Frost. (978-1-63555-100-6)

Heart of the Devil by Ali Vali. We know most of Cain and Emma Casey's story, but *Heart of the Devil* will take you back to where it began one fateful night with a tray loaded with beer. (978-1-63555-045-0)

Known Threat by Kara A. McLeod. When Special Agent Ryan O'Connor reluctantly questions who protects the Secret Service, she learns courage truly is found in unlikely places. Agent O'Connor Series #3. (978-1-63555-132-7)

Seer and the Shield by D. Jackson Leigh. Time is running out for the Dragon Horse Army while two unlikely heroines struggle to put aside their attraction and find a way to stop a deadly cult. Dragon Horse War, Book 3. (978-1-63555-170-9)

Sinister Justice by Steve Pickens. When a vigilante targets citizens of Jake Finnigan's hometown, Jake and his partner Sam fall under suspicion themselves as they investigate the murders. (978-1-63555-094-8)

The Universe Between Us by Jane C. Esther. Ana Mitchell must make the hardest choice of her life: the promise of new love Jolie Dann on Earth, or a humanity-saving mission to colonize Mars. (978-1-63555-106-8)

Touch by Kris Bryant. Can one touch heal a heart? (978-1-63555-084-9)